## *Contents*

| | | |
|---|---|---|
| Chapter 1 | And Then There Was One | 5 |
| Chapter 2 | The Three-legged Haggis | 12 |
| Chapter 3 | Breakfast at Devil's Maze | 18 |
| Chapter 4 | Loo Roll Confetti | 29 |
| Chapter 5 | The Dark Witches' Lair | 38 |
| Chapter 6 | Tweezel Berries | 48 |
| Chapter 7 | Body Pumps | 57 |
| Chapter 8 | Dead Souls Waking | 65 |
| Chapter 9 | Number One Goatfell | 74 |
| Chapter 10 | The Watcher | 86 |
| Chapter 11 | The Sleeping Gardener | 91 |
| Chapter 12 | Book Shower | 98 |
| Chapter 13 | Attack of the Thistle Pixies | 103 |
| Chapter 14 | Groucho's Gauntlet | 113 |
| Chapter 15 | Hidden in the Clouds | 124 |
| Chapter 16 | Fairy Dew | 129 |
| Chapter 17 | Assault on Brodick | 134 |
| Chapter 18 | Bridge 'Club' | 139 |
| Chapter 19 | Mogdred's Vow | 146 |

## Chapter 1

## *And Then There Was One*

Sparkling blue light filled the cave as sunshine reflected off the sapphire crystals that had been lovingly hung from every single stalactite by Morven, the beautiful Sea Dragon who lived there. Her scales shimmered in ever-changing shades of violet and indigo.

It was early evening and Morven was standing over a huge pot in the part of the cave she used as a kitchen because water dripped in from a small hole in the ceiling above. She had once placed the carcass of a little rowing boat under the hole to collect the drips and realised it made the perfect kitchen sink!

Morven was adding various ingredients to the pot, picking them up gently with her teeth and dropping them in. The dish she was so carefully preparing was seaweed stew. A rare treat, because the luminous seaweed needed to make the stew was almost impossible to find, as it only grew in the dark depths of Domhain Loch.

Into the pot went gammell roots. The gammell roots didn't look very appetising. They had thick, black, prickly skin and the smell from them was disgusting. Just like rotting fish!

Morven picked up a few at a time between her teeth and squeezed gently until their pale pink flesh popped out from their skin. As the flesh appeared, she dropped them into the pot. The vegetables tasted nothing like the way they smelled. After shedding their scary looking skin, the pink flesh inside was soft and sweet, with a citrus aroma.

'One for me, one for the pot. One for me, one for the pot,' Morven hummed as she munched her way through half of the huge pile of gammell roots while dropping the other half into the stew.

She started adding spices to season the dish, discussing the merits or otherwise with herself as she went along.

'Mm, a touch more fire chilli I think? Maybe a tad more? Just a snitch more.' She stuck her tongue into the pot… 'Perfect!' she muttered, slurping down a mouthful of stew.

The dragon's home was surprisingly bright and airy, due to a hole in the ceiling near the back of the cave which allowed sunlight to come streaming through.

Despite the brightness, Morven's eyelids felt very heavy. They were drooping halfway down and every now and then she'd find herself standing upright with her eyes completely closed, at which point she would wake up, startled, and give herself a shake. A loud grumbling growl that periodically echoed around the cave walls was also helping to keep her awake. The growls were coming from the bottom of her stomach. Morven had been trawling Domhain Loch all day, looking for luminous seaweed for the stew. And now she was tired and hungry.

Morven and her husband, Tavish, were two of the last

remaining Sea Dragons on earth. They had fled to the Isle of Arran, home of Lizzie the Protector, to raise a family. Their first child was still an egg and the precious bundle was due to hatch in just a few weeks. The dark-grey, stripy markings on the shell meant it was a boy.

Morven had been preparing the cave for the new arrival for weeks. She had gathered glistening stones, fluffy wool balls and teething toys made from an array of seashells, rocks and pebbles.

Most importantly, she had been making the baby pool. When they hatch, baby Sea Dragons need to stay submerged in fresh water until all of their scales have fully formed, and this can take up to three months. Morven had dug out a large ditch at the back of the cave to make sure the pool had lots of sunlight. She had lined the pool with clay from the bottom of Domhain Loch and filled it with fresh water from the loch. Everything was ready.

Morven was so excited she couldn't help but smile every time she thought of tiny dragon feet pattering about the cave. But, she was also fearful for her precious little bundle, as she knew that if Mogdred ever found out about the egg, she would do everything in her power to destroy it.

'Tavish should be home any time now,' Morven said aloud to herself.

Gripping with her teeth, she picked up the two massive pieces of slate they used as plates and placed them on the great stone table that stood in the centre of the cave. Next, she took the pot in her mouth and poured huge dollops of seaweed stew onto each of the slates. The luminous seaweed glowed, its yellowish-orange shimmer replacing the blue sparkles, which had mostly disappeared now that the sun had almost set.

Morven had been so preoccupied with making dinner that she got quite a shock when she realised how much the daylight was dimming. As quickly as she could, she began to ignite the dozens of torches set on ledges around the cave, puffing gently on each one until the twine inside burst into flames. Within a few minutes her home was so brightly illuminated you could easily think it was midday and not seven o'clock in the evening. Morven never allowed the cave to fall into complete darkness, especially at night, as that was when the Night Witches were on patrol, looking to attack any unsuspecting victims.

Wondering where on earth Tavish could have got to, Morven decided to eat her helping of stew. An hour passed, then another, and Morven fell asleep. With her mouth wide open, she was snoring so loudly that the sapphire crystals hung all around the cave swayed to and fro, making a soothing, tinkling sound as they chimed against each other. This was the perfect environment for a baby to fall asleep… and its mummy!

In the middle of a lovely dream in which her egg had hatched into a baby Sea dragon, Morven rolled over onto her tummy. As she did so, the tip of her tail hit one of the stalactites growing from the roof of the cave, sending sapphire crystals crashing to the ground. Morven jumped up, startled by the noise and looked around in a sleepy haze.

The first thing she realised was that Tavish still hadn't returned home!

Morven began to get really worried. Tavish always made sure he was home before nightfall, especially since the Night Witch attacks had started.

She went over to the pile of straw neatly packed at

the back of the cave and stared adoringly at the fragile little egg that had been placed there. Using her mouth, she carefully transferred it into the baby pool. Once she had made sure that the egg was fully submerged, she gathered twigs and branches in her jaws and placed them in a criss-cross pattern over the pool. When it was completely covered, she took a deep breath and blew dust over the makeshift cover until it blended in with the rest of the floor.

Just then, an enormous gust of wind surged through the cave, extinguishing every one of the torches she had lit earlier and throwing her to the ground.

There was not a single shred of light anywhere. Morven blinked frantically, her large green eyes trying to adjust to the pitch black.

Then, she heard Tavish crying out to her through the darkness.

'Run Morven, run!' he yelled. 'They've taken the McDuffs – we're the last... R*uuun*.'

The dreadful, piercing screams she heard coming from the direction of the entrance to the cave unnerved Morven. She tried to force her legs to move but they were rooted to the spot. As she struggled to move, a lightning bolt came hurtling towards her. It skimmed her shoulder, only just missing her head.

'How's that for starters?' howled Gretch with a hideous shriek of laughter, sending another assault of lightning bolts towards Morven.

Gretch was the daughter of Mogdred, the most evil and feared of all the Night Witches. But Mogdred had been blinded during her last battle against Lizzie the Protector and in order to guard herself from harm until her eyesight recovered, Mogdred had ordered that every Sea Dragon be killed. The reason for this is because Sea Dragons breathe out water which is so pure it can melt the black soul of a Night Witch, destroying it instantly.

Mounted on her broom, Gretch looked down gleefully as she swooped over the body of the male Sea Dragon. Her lightning bolt had made a direct hit. Mogdred would be pleased!

Gretch decided to land, but her huge stomach touched the ground before her feet could reach it, causing her broom to tip up at the back. The front dug into the ground like a javelin pole and sent her careering across the floor of the cave, wobbling like a jelly. When she finally stopped, she found it very hard to get back onto her feet. She had to roll onto her hands and knees, push her enormous bottom up in the air, then place each of her feet firmly on the ground, before managing to push up into a standing position.

Gretch was five feet tall, but her legs were only one foot long. They had shrunk down from carrying her enormous body around. She wore black tights and a black smock that barely covered her stomach. Her skin was such a dark shade of grey that it was almost black and on her face it hung down so much it looked as though it belonged to someone with a much bigger head. She had short black hair congealed with grease from never being washed and long hooked nails with ragged edges… good for ripping things apart!

Just as she entered the cave, Gretch's twin sister, Sloth, landed with a splat a few centimetres in front of her. A mirror image of Gretch, she too had been pole-vaulted off of her broom.

'Oi, watch out, you big lump!' Gretch complained.

'Oh, stop your whinging,' Sloth sniped back. 'We need to find the female Sea Dragon. C'mon, she can't be far away.'

The two sisters waddled into the cave side by side.

Gretch's first lightning bolt had acted like an adrenalin punch when it hit Morven, sending a rush of energy from her shoulder all the way down into her powerful legs. Although she couldn't see, at least she could move again.

Picturing in her mind a massive boulder that sat against the cave wall opposite her giant stone dining table, Morven ran straight towards it. As the tip of her nose made contact with the rock, she opened her jaws wide and blasted out a massive water jet. The boulder disintegrated immediately, revealing a secret exit. Tavish's last screams echoing in her head, Morven pushed through the large opening, spread her magnificent wings and disappeared beyond the clouds high above the cave.

Finding no more dragons in the cave, Sloth and Gretch soon grew bored and left to tell Mogdred all about how they had killed Tavish.

## Chapter 2

## *The Three-legged Haggis*

McCools' door shuddered with each huge knock. 'It must be someone or something very big,' he thought as the hinges started to creak and splinters landed at his stubby toes. The banging was getting so loud he was sure the door wouldn't hold out much longer.

Morven had never met McCools before, but she knew of him. A recluse who lived at the top of Goatfell mountain, he was reputed to be the wisest creature on Arran. If anyone knew how to help her, it would be him.

The house was tall, thin and crooked with a chimney stack in the rough outline of a teapot right at the top. The whole building was pure white, including the roof and chimney, so that it blended into the snow-capped mountain. In fact, if it wasn't for the bright red door, you wouldn't see the strange little house at all!

McCools had moved to Goatfell many years before to get away from the Humans, who were rather partial to dining on Haggis and a strange vegetable called neaps. In fact, the Humans seemed to like it so much, they would

*McCools*

actually say a speech before they ate it!

McCools had fled to a part of the mountain that couldn't be reached by Humans. His house was perched on a cliff face that was covered in snow for eleven and a half months of the year. Even during the two weeks of summer it was too dangerous for climbers to get to, as the melting snow would avalanche down the cliff, taking any nosey parkers with it.

For most of the year, the house was only accessible by air. But not by plane or helicopter – there wasn't anywhere for these machines to land. It could only be reached by birds and other flying creatures, such as dragons.

'Please help me,' Morven pleaded through the closed door. 'We are the last of our kind and we need your help.'

McCools immediately realised the voice must belong to a Sea Dragon. Like his kind, they had been hunted to near extinction. Only, instead of being hounded down by a bunch of Humans bearing pitch-forks, they had been stalked by Mogdred and her deadly army of Night Witches.

McCools opened the door. Morven's wings wouldn't fit through the opening, so she stayed outside and bent her head low to take a closer look at him. He was tiny compared to her, only half a metre tall. He looked like a little ball covered in bright orange fur, with three legs sticking out below and two arms that stuck out either side of his round body. His arms and legs were also orange, but rather than being covered in fur they were smooth and soft, like the skin on a baby's bottom.

'So this is what a Haggis looks like,' she thought. Just by looking into his big purple eyes, she knew she could trust this wee three-legged creature. He oozed kindness.

Morven tried to speak, but every time she thought about what had happened, tears poured down her cheeks. It was as though she was in a nightmare that she couldn't wake up from.

'The... the... the... *dead*. They... they... all *dead*,' she stuttered.

Shaking uncontrollably, she kept repeating the same words over and over.

McCools produced a green herb from a fold in the tartan scarf he wore around his neck.

'You're in shock. This will help,' he said in a low voice. 'Open your mouth.'

Morven opened her huge jaws and McCools placed a few little leaves onto her tongue.

Within seconds, she had stopped shaking and found she could breathe properly again, although she was still in incredible pain. It was a sharp, constant pain, as if her heart was going to burst. With a huge effort, she managed to tell McCools everything that had happened, including how she had hidden the egg.

'I don't understand,' she wept. 'I thought we would be safe on Arran.'

'Mogdred has been injured,' McCools explained gently. 'The Night Witches are scared and they have been ordered to kill any creature that might be able to harm her.'

'But what about Lizzie the Protector? Can't she stop them?'

'I'm so sorry, Morven.' McCools' eyes filled with grief. 'Lizzie is dead.' There was a pause as he choked back his tears. 'There's no one to stop the Night Witches now.'

Morven could not believe what she was hearing. All was lost. Lizzie was dead, like her dear Tavish. And she had no idea if her egg was safe or not.

'Morven!' McCools' sharp tone broke into her thoughts. 'You must go back. The witches don't know about the egg, so they will not be looking for it. You must take it and place it in the deepest part of Domhain Loch. Your baby will be safe there. The Night Witches wouldn't dare go near a freshwater loch... not even on patrol.'

Without another word, Morven stretched out her immense wings and flew back up into the sky, heading towards the cave. She was travelling as fast as her mighty wings could take her.

As she took off McCools shouted after her, 'No... no... they're in the clouds.'

But Morven could only hear the thrashing of the wind against her wings as they beat through the air. She could not hear the bolts of lightning hurtling towards her from the dark clouds above.

Three of the bolts hit her left wing, which instantly burst into flames, but on she flew. She kept going as though the bolts hadn't even touched her. Another hit her back, then another. But they didn't slow her pace. She was a mother on a mission, determined to save her child.

Two Night Witches came flying towards her, casting a death spell. Morven fired back with a huge water spray, and partway through chanting, the witches began to melt. Their skin bubbled up, then their bodies started to lose their shape. It was like watching a chocolate bar morph into a mud puddle. After a few seconds, black slime was all that was left of the Night Witches. It dripped from their brooms, now flying out of control without their pilots, heading towards the water below.

Morven swung her head around and sprayed the Night Witches coming at her from behind. The five cackling creatures vaporised instantly as the water spray soaked their black skin.

She flew down to the loch below and dragged her injured wing through the cold water. The flames died down to reveal scorched skin that was barely clinging to her tired and beaten skeleton.

Taking off once more, Morven flew low and silent, concealed in the mist that covered the sea like a blanket. She stopped half a mile from the cave and looked around. There was no sign of the Night Witches.

Morven sank into the water until she was completely immersed, and waited. All night long she lay under the water and when the sun rose in the morning she emerged like an immense Water Phoenix, her strength restored by the healing powers of the loch. For the first time she could see the devastation around the cave. The black smoke still drifting through the air carried a horrible stench.

Spreading her wings, she flew towards the entrance to the cave, but when she got there she sensed that something was wrong... *It was ALL wrong*! As she trod slowly through the burning rubble, she knew she was probably walking into a trap.

The cave was still in complete darkness, even though it was morning. Every crack had been covered so that not even the slightest shred of light could penetrate the pitch black. And the air stank... of Night Witch!

Suddenly, a lightning bolt came hurtling towards Morven. It passed through the back of the cave, lighting it up for a split second as it sped towards her chest.

That second was all it took for her to see that the floor of the cave hadn't been disturbed. Her egg was safe.

Morven collapsed to the ground, as she took her last breath.

## Chapter 3

## *Breakfast at Devil's Maze*

Lily woke up super early. The sky was still, and not a creature, flower or insect could be heard outside. She waited as long as she could before opening her eyes, but as soon as she opened them, she was wide awake. She jumped out of bed and started racing around her room.

She was mega-excited because it was her birthday. This was Lily's ninety-sixth birthday. But as Flower Nymphs celebrate their birthday every month, she was actually only eight in human years.

Lily's birth had been a day of joy and sadness. She was born on the same day the Night Witches had murdered Morven and Tavish, the last remaining Sea Dragons. Every year at midnight, the Flower Nymphs would gather at the cave where Morven and Tavish had been killed to pay their respects, and also to remember that evil could strike again, at any time!

Lily peeled back the pale pink petals that acted like curtains in her giant water lily bedroom and tried to

*Buttercup*

decide if it was too early to head out. She was desperate to see her friends, Blade and Buttercup, to find out what amazing present they had for her. Every birthday, the three friends would surprise one another with a fantastic gift. For Lily's last birthday, her friends had made a harness out of long water reeds, so that Lily could ride a dragonfly.

The three friends had gone to the pond, and Boris, the biggest dragonfly in the castle grounds, had agreed to let Lily ride him. Well, not exactly! Boris wasn't the sharpest tack in the box. So when none of the other dragonflies agreed to a harness made from water reeds to be wrapped around their back and being sat on by a Flower Nymph for her birthday joy-ride, Buttercup had come up with a plan!

Buttercup knew Boris was very vain and she decided to use this to her advantage.

'Hey, who's strongest dragonfly on the pond?' she hollered from the side of the water.

'That would be me!' Boris replied in a confident, military style tone.

'Yeah, you do look pretty strong, but I don't think you're as strong as me!'

Buttercup turned to fly off.

'What on earth makes you say that?' Boris retorted in a high-pitched shriek. He couldn't believe the little nymph could possibly think that she was stronger than him.

He was hovering above Lily, his wings racing at a hundred miles per hour. He couldn't contain his frustration, and the more annoyed he became, the faster his wings flapped.

She turned back and stated, quite matter of fact, 'Well, I've heard you can't carry someone your own weight. Whereas, Flower Nymphs can easily carry one another!'

'That's just not true,' spluttered Boris, as tiny sparks started to appear around the edges of his wings they were flapping so fast.

'Prove it then,' challenged Buttercup. 'Let's see if you can carry Lily.'

Without thinking, Boris allowed Lily to strap her harness onto his back and fly around on him for thirty minutes!

Afterwards, all three friends agreed that Boris was indeed the strongest dragonfly on the pond. He was so pleased, he proceeded to let Blade and Buttercup both have a ride on his back too.

Thinking about all the fun she'd had flying with Boris just made Lily even more excited. She had to get out of there! So she quickly fluttered down to the pond to get washed.

She dipped her fingers into the water and began to wiggle them. Then she put in her hands and waved them about. After she pulled her hands out, she popped her feet in. The freezing cold water gave her goosebumps up and down her legs. Next, she put her face into the water and shook her head from side to side. Brr… it was so cold, she began shrugging her shoulders. Last, but not least, she skimmed across the top of the water with the tips of her wings.

'Phew, I'm glad that's over,' she thought to herself. 'Now for hair grooming… Yuk!'

Lily had long white hair that trailed along the ground whenever she walked, which wasn't very often. This is because Flower Nymphs usually flutter wherever they go. Fluttering is similar to flying, except a bit more erratic. The nymphs have eight tiny wings that flap really quickly, creating an air cushion underneath them. The Flower Nymphs are so light, the air cushion lifts them up off the ground. It's a bit bumpy, as the air cushion can be blown by the wind in any direction. This is why people often say that Flower Nymphs head wherever the wind takes them!

Every now and then, there is a big dip that sends the Flower Nymph plunging towards the ground, spiralling out of control. This usually happens when they pass over something cold, which is why Lily was always on the lookout for icicles or frozen puddles. Lily was no fragile little Flower Nymph, she was more of a daredevil. She loved nothing better than to dive-bomb towards the ground, spinning all the way, then, at the last minute, she'd flap her wings super-fast to lift up, to avoid splattering into the ground.

Although Lily was just three centimetres tall, it was still really difficult for her to comb her hair, because she couldn't reach the ends. She fluttered through the garden until she spotted an acorn hidden under a bed of leaves. She grabbed onto it with both hands, then shook her head frantically into the centre of the acorn until her long white hair became twisted and entwined in the acorn. She then fluttered as fast as she could through the air until the acorn shook loose and fell to the ground, leaving her long hair shiny and untangled.

'Ah, all groomed. It is *definitely* time to wake up the others,' thought Lily, and she headed towards the rose bushes.

Huge puddles of saliva were gathering at Torgle's feet. The gooey green gunk trickled down his chin and dripped onto the grass, making it slimy and muddy underfoot. He had been sitting very still at the edge of the pond so as not to scare away any unsuspecting flies, when he noticed

*Torgle*

Lily carrying out her morning cleaning ritual. He watched her through his big, round, red eyes and he couldn't help smacking his lips. Normally, the greedy toad would have flies for breakfast, or perhaps a few slugs. But today, Torgle was going to have Flower Nymph...

'Mm, how delicious,' he thought.

Torgle crept quietly through the long grass, keeping a safe distance behind Lily, who was now flying all over the place. One minute heading left, then right, then spiralling towards the ground out of control. Just seconds before crash-landing face-first, she'd flick her head back, turn her whole body round one hundred and eighty degrees and be aiming for the sky again. Then the whole display would start once more!

'A most peculiar way to fly,' thought Torgle.

But then again, there were a lot of very peculiar things about Flower Nymphs. This is the reason he was staying a good distance behind Lily. Many of the creatures in the gardens spoke about the secret powers of the Flower Nymphs. So Torgle decided to spy on Lily a little longer, before eating her!

He didn't want to take any chances in case the stories of the nymphs' special powers were true. Although, he really couldn't see how it could be difficult to capture this tiny creature and scoff her for his breakfast. She looked so frail as she bounced through the air, pushed from one air current to another. She seemed to be heading for the rose-beds, so he followed on, being very careful not to be seen. 'Maybe she is going to meet another Flower Nymph? Then I could have nymph for breakfast and lunch,' Torgle thought greedily.

There was a giant maze between the lily pond and

the rose-beds. Humans called it the Devil's Maze – not because there was some devil lurking inside the maze, but because they would say, 'It's a devil to get out of the maze!'

Humans could get lost inside the maze for hours, or even days. One actually got lost for ten days and when he reappeared, he couldn't remember anything that had happened to him. Although, he did keep babbling on about being chased by a walking bush! The other humans just assumed he had gone a little mad after being inside the maze for so long, and that he must have started hallucinating – seeing things that were all just inside his head.

As soon as Lily entered the maze, she fluttered down to the ground and started to walk, dragging her long hair behind her. Twigs and dirt clung to the long white strands of hair, which really annoyed Lily. Especially as she had just combed it! She was stomping her feet in annoyance as she walked through the little mouse-holes that had been cut into the bottom of the hedges which formed the maze. The holes were dotted along a dirt path that went from one end of the maze to the other, in an almost straight line. The path was so tiny, only someone really small could use it.

Lily did not like walking, especially when it got her hair dirty. But the maze had been enchanted many years earlier by a mischievous elf who loved to watch people get lost there. So that he could have some fun, the elf had cast a spell of 'gravitation', which meant that if anyone tried to fly through the maze or climb up the sides, they would be pulled back towards the ground, like a piece of metal attracted by a giant magnet. The elf would sit high up in the maze, laughing as he watched people twisting and turning as they struggled to escape from the invisible force that was pulling them back towards the ground.

Torgle could barely get his chubby brown frame through the tiny mouse-holes. He only managed because his entire body was covered in gooey, green slime that acted like a lubricant, allowing him to squeeze through the holes, one layer of tummy at a time. Torgle was now even more annoyed than Lily at the maze and decided he'd had enough. It was now time for breakfast!

Lily walked through the last hole and emerged at the far side of the maze, right at the foot of the rose-beds. She started to flutter from bud to bud, checking inside each one, trying to find Blade. She was so busy searching for Blade, she didn't notice Torgle's long, black tongue coming straight at her like a whip.

The tongue wrapped itself twice around her waist.

Lily couldn't breathe. She gasped for air, but nothing could reach her lungs past the tight rope of Torgle's tongue. It felt as though all of the air had been sucked out of her body. She grabbed Torgle's tongue, but it just wrapped itself round her tighter with every grasp.

The long tongue started to curl back in, pulling Lily towards Torgle's wide-open mouth. His red eyes glistened with glee as he watched the tiny nymph's body being drawn closer and closer. She was almost at his lips, so close he could smell the sweet scent of a lily flower.

'Mmm, delicious,' he drooled. 'You will be even tastier than I imagined.'

Lily could feel cold slime dripping from Torgle's jaws onto her wings and arms. She was shivering all over. She opened her mouth to scream.

'No point in screaming, my little flower. There's no

one here to help you,' sniggered Torgle.

It was over in a flash. Torgle's tongue recoiled into his mouth and Lily was gone.

Torgle ran his long, black tongue around his thick, brown lips, smacking them with satisfaction, when suddenly he doubled over, grabbing hold of his stomach, and began to retch.

'*Bluuugh.*'

Thick, warm, green-brown mucous started spewing through the air, projected like water from a hose. Lily hurtled through the vomit, covered in slime and half-digested bugs. Torgle's eyes were bulging out of his head. They were no longer glistening with glee, but pouring painful tears.

He fell to the ground and started rolling from side to side, choking and coughing at the same time, his hands clenched around his throat.

'What have you done?' he screeched.

'Naughty, naughty Little Froggy,' thought Lily. 'We don't taste as good as we look… do we?'

'Answer me, you horrible little nymph,' demanded Torgle.

But Lily didn't answer. She just stared at him as she floated a few centimetres off the ground, fluttering her wings. Torgle realised that the stories of the Flower Nymphs must be true after all. Lily had poisoned him with a venomous pollen spray.

'She hadn't been opening her mouth to scream. She was opening her mouth to spray toxic pollen down my throat!' thought Torgle, now feeling very afraid.

He rolled onto his tummy as fast as his rotund waistline would let him, then started pushing back with his hands as hard as he could. He slid his fat body backwards, towards the maze. Lily fluttered just above him, staring into his eyes the whole time. 'Bye bye, Little Froggy,' she hummed to herself as Torgle started to disappear back into the maze.

When the last part of Torgle's tummy had finally squeezed back through the hedge into the maze, Lily resumed her search. She looked inside every single bud, but there was no sign of Blade anywhere.

'That's strange, thought Lily. Blade is never awake this early. But not to worry. I'll go and find Buttercup instead. I'm sure she'll still be asleep!' And off she fluttered towards the carpet of bright yellow flowers at the foot of Brodick Castle.

'Hello Torgle.'

The warm tones of the woman's voice were soothing and gentle. Torgle was still spitting out the pollen from his mouth as he glared up to see the most beautiful creature standing over him. She was at least seven feet tall and her magnificent antlers were entwined with long, flowing, purple hair. She trotted slowly towards him, revealing her hybrid body – a human torso perched upon deer legs.

'I've been watching you,' she whispered. Her tone was still gentle, but now it sent a cold chill down his spine.

'What now?' thought Torgle, with a feeling of dread.

'I have a proposition for you,' she continued in an eerie whisper.

After the morning he had just endured, Torgle was in no mood for 'propositions'!

'And what if I'm not interested in your *proposition?*' he croaked back sharply.

'Then I'm afraid I'll have to finish what *you* started,' said the woman.

Torgle stared back at her with a blank expression.

'Why, breakfast at Devil's Maze, of course… with *you* as the main course this time!' she smiled.

Admittedly, this would not be Serena's first choice for a healthy start to the day. But, needs must!

Thankfully, she could see from the look of terror in Torgle's eyes that she would not be dining on toad after all. Well, not today anyway!

## Chapter 4

## *Loo Roll Confetti*

Almost an hour had passed and Thumble Tumble still couldn't think of an idea for a present. Her toes were all wrinkly, because her feet had been dangling in the loch for so long.

'We need to think of something really awesome, Jock. Flower Nymphs always have amazing parties and even more amazing gifts!'

Jock didn't answer. His mind was elsewhere. It was eight years to the day that his parents had been murdered by Night Witches. He was just an egg when they were killed. The Deer folk had taken him from the pool where his mother had left him and hidden him in the depths of Domhain Loch. For the past eight years, the Deer Folk had protected Jock by keeping him hidden and making up stories about the Ollpheist to keep people away.

They spread tales about a hideous, four-headed monster that trawled Domhain Loch looking for unsuspecting victims to feast on, so that everyone would be too scared to go into the loch.

Jock had grown up sad and alone, with only the occasional visit from the Deer Folk for company.

All that had changed five months ago when he met Thumble Tumble. Together, they had battled with the Night Witches to save the Deer Folk, and Thumble Tumble had been presented with the winner's trophy from the Great Games, the Lazlo Cup.

Jock was staring deep into the loch, daydreaming about what it would be like to be celebrating his birthday with his parents by his side.

Although he had never seen them, he knew in his heart what they looked like. His father, an immense creature with shiny black scales and razor-sharp spikes all the way down his back and along the edge of his wings. His mother, slightly smaller, although still a huge figure of a dragon, her scales in tones of indigo and violet, changing from one colour to the other in the sunlight.

The ripples caused by Thumble Tumble's paddling feet were hypnotic. So much so, Jock was sure he could see his parents standing on either side of his reflection in the water. He smiled up as they leaned towards him. But before they could wrap their huge wings around him and give him the loving hug he had been longing for, the reflection started to break up. At first cracks appeared in the centre of his face. They then spread out breaking the reflection into tiny pieces before it disappeared in a surge of ripples.

'What did you do that for?' he snapped.

Thumble Tumble looked blankly at Jock as she continued to pull her feet out of the loch.

'Do what?' she asked.

Jock realised that Thumble Tumble hadn't seen the

same image as he had in the water.

'I'm sorry,' he apologised. 'It's just that I always find *this* day really difficult. Even after eight years!'

Thumble Tumble knew how hard it must be for Jock, which is why she had been trying to distract him all morning by gibbering on about Lily's birthday present.

But when she had seen him staring into the loch, the look of grief in his eyes filled her with sorrow. She *had* to do something to help him, which is why she had enchanted the loch with a 'Hearts Desire' spell. This let him see for just a few moments what a birthday with his parents would be like.

Thumble Tumble was forbidden from casting this type of spell, as it could cause more harm than good. And this was a perfect example! The spell had ended too soon, so Jock never got the loving hug he so desperately desired. Instead, he was left feeling emptier inside than ever!

Thumble Tumble's glum expression gave away how terrible she felt that the spell had gone so horribly wrong.

'Hey, misery guts,' said Jock, sounding much perkier. 'I said I was sorry. Now let's get down to business. What about honey wine? That would make a pretty awesome gift.'

Thumble Tumble shook her head.

'*She's a Flower Nymph!* They can have Honey Wine whenever they want,' she replied in a brattish tone.

'OK, how about Scoffalicious Chocolate? Flower Nymphs don't have that every day of the week,' said Jock, feeling rather pleased with himself for coming up with such a good suggestion.

'Nope, but I gave her a huge batch for her birthday last year,' sighed Thumble Tumble, raising her eyebrows as though Jock should have known this – even though he didn't actually know Thumble Tumble a year ago.

'Hmm… I know!' Jock's eyes opened wide and he started grinning like a Cheshire Cat. 'Nectar Candy Canes!'

'Oh for goodness sake, Jock. Don't you know anything about Flower Nymphs? They *make* the Nectar Candy Canes!'

'I'm so terribly sorry,' Jock said sarcastically. 'As it happens, I don't really know anything about Flower Nymphs. Except that it seems there isn't anything they can't get for themselves!'

'Yes!' hollered Thumble Tumble, as if she'd just come first in a bubble-blowing competition. 'That's it – something they can't get for themselves! You're a genius, Jock!'

Jock wasn't overwhelmed with joy at Thumble Tumble's announcement. Just confused!

'They love tweezel berry juice, but hate Devil's Maze!' Thumble Tumble continued excitedly.

'I'm not quite getting the connection,' said Jock, still completely in the dark.

'Well, you need tweezel berries for the juice, and the tweezel berry bush can only be found in the Devil's Maze,' Thumble Tumble said, quite matter of fact.

'*And*?' said Jock, now feeling more frustrated than ever.

Thumble Tumble realised she'd need to tell Jock the full story of Devil's Maze for him to get it. So she began:

It all started about fifty years ago with an elf called Minx. Minx was an accountant for E.L.F.S. & Co.

His father was also an accountant for E.L.F.S., along with his grandfather and his father before him.

It was just another day like every other day in Minx's boring life. Minx woke up at seven a.m. to the sound of his beetle alarm screeching at the top of the little bug's lungs. He then spent the next thirty minutes trying to convince his legs to wake up too.

When he eventually managed to drag himself out of bed he headed to the shower, where he would have the next battle of the morning, this time with his hair. He had a huge bush of red, wiry hair, which was almost impossible to get the soap out of. Finally, he put on a crisp white shirt and his MacDonald tartan kilt, then headed off to work.

At almost one metre, Minx was tall for an elf. He had oversized hairy feet and his large green eyes were oval in shape, with thick, red eyebrows half covering them.

On his way to work Minx picked up the *Elf and Gnome Daily News* and an extra sweet double choco lattè from the coffee bar.

That's where he saw her for the first time. She was a vision of beauty, the most stunning elf in the world, standing only a few feet away from him.

Selfie had long, blonde hair that flowed when she walked, like a silk scarf blowing in the wind. Her eyes were so blue that Minx felt as if he could dive right into them… or was that the shine off of the blue pearls wrapped around her neck?

Selfie was smart, rich and totally gorgeous. And she knew it!

After visiting the coffee bar every single day for

weeks, Minx finally built up the courage to ask her out on a date. He couldn't believe his ears when she agreed to go out with him.

It wasn't long before wedding plans were being made.

It would be the most talked about wedding of the decade. The wedding of the beautiful socialite Selfie to… somebody!

The paparazzi turned up in droves. Every gossip magazine, from *Scorching* to *Hiya*, had a reporter at the high society event. There would be celebs from all over. Elves, witches, fairies, nymphs and an array of other mystical creatures, all dressed in their glitziest outfits, trying to outdo one another.

Photographers hid everywhere in an attempt to get that 'special snap'. Eight had taken up residence in the eaves of the church, three were hiding in the aisles, and one over-keen photographer had even paid a large lady ogre to let him hide under her puffball skirt.

As the ogre's seat was right in front of the altar, it seemed the perfect hideout to get some great pictures. The only downside was that she suffered from wind, and an ogre's wind is pretty repulsive! After just five minutes, the photographer fainted from the fumes and so didn't manage to get even a single shot of the day's events.

All of the photographers were looking for that 'one' snap that would bring them fame and fortune. Just like the very celebrities they were stalking, ironically!

A perfect photo would be to catch the bride picking her nose on camera. Or even better, scratching her bottom. Alternatively, perhaps the groom would trip on the dance floor? Not quite as good, but still worth a pretty penny.

They could never have imagined the field day they were about to have!

Minx arrived at the church with his best friend, Griff. He had invited all his friends and his entire family, including those remote family members he didn't really know. Like his fourth cousin, Fornte Radnor something or other, from his mum's side of the family. An odd looking fellow with beady yellow eyes and a chin that stuck out like a doorstep. Fornte was the very last guest to be seated.

The church was heaving, with the guests and paparazzi crammed in like sardines. Minx stood at the altar with a huge grin on his face. He had to keep pinching himself every few minutes to make sure it was real.

The wedding march sounded and confetti started pouring down from the balconies above.

'Strange looking confetti,' thought Griff. 'Looks more like loo roll!'

When the eggs started landing at his feet, Griff realised he'd been right the first time... it *was* loo roll!

Minx looked up to see a full row of beautiful elves launching eggs and loo roll from the balcony above his head. It was only at that instant he noticed that none of Selfie's friends or family were in the church.

He couldn't believe what was happening. *Why?* His whole world was dissolving around him. *How could she do this?* His heart was pounding in his chest as he shouted, 'What's going on?'

'OMG,' Selfie smirked back, arrogant as a prima-donna popstar. 'You didn't *really* think I would stoop so low, did you? It's April Fool's Day!'

Then all of the beautiful elves surrounding her began laughing uncontrollably.

Minx hadn't given the date a second thought. He had been too in love to notice what day of the week it was.

He ran from the church, barely able to hold back the tears. As soon as he was through the front door, the flood-gates opened. Tears streaming from his eyes and nose, he kept running until he found himself in a giant maze. '*Perfect...*' he thought, '...for getting lost in!'

The whole ordeal changed Minx for the worse. He enchanted the maze with a Spell of Gravitation that dragged people back to the ground if they tried to fly or climb out. This was so that he could sit high up in the bushes and watch them squirm as they tried to break free from the gravitational pull. Just the same way he had squirmed that day.

Selfie changed too. She instantly regretted what she had done. In fact, she had actually fallen in love with Minx, but she was *so* selfish she couldn't even bear to share her heart with someone else. So she had hatched a cruel plan to make sure Minx would fall out of love with her... and the plan worked!

Nothing has been seen of Selfie or Minx since that fateful day, and over the years the maze became known as 'Devil's Maze', because it is so difficult to find a way back out of it.

And that's the story of Devil's Maze,' said Thumble Tumble.

*Jock*

'I'm still not quite sure where the Flower Nymphs and the tweezel berries fit in to all of this,' said Jock hesitantly.

'Flower Nymphs hate walking,' replied Thumble Tumble in a rather annoying I-told-you-so voice. 'They have to *walk* through the maze because of the gravitation spell, and this gets their hair filthy. They cannot stand having dirty hair, so they hardly ever go through Devil's Maze – but that's the only place where you can find the tweezel berry bush.'

'Ah!' said Jock, finally catching on.

## Chapter 5

## The Dark Witches' Lair

Buttercup and Blade had been in the kitchen for hours. They were both very hot and sweaty from the heat coming off of the cast iron oven.

'That's layer number five all decorated,' said Blade with a look of satisfaction. His bright green face, glistened with beads of sweat forming a conga across his cheeks.

Like all Flower Nymphs, he was three centimetres tall and had eight delicate wings on his back. The wings were so fine they looked as though they were made out of cobwebs.

However, unlike his friends Lily and Buttercup, who had beautifully smooth skin, Blade was covered from head to toe in tiny pimples. These pimples morphed into razor-sharp thorns every time he felt threatened or in danger.

In fact, Blade's real name was Thorn. But he didn't like being called Thorn and refused point-blank to answer to Thorn. Instead, he had renamed himself Blade!

As well as being razor-sharp, the thorns that covered Blade's body were laced with a powerful poison. The poison from two thorns was strong enough to take out a man; four or five could take down a giant!

Blade was quite unassuming and certainly didn't look very dangerous, with his tiny green physique and bright red hair spiralling out from the roots.

'Only two more to go,' said Buttercup, in a cheerful chirp.

'Do we *really* need to make a seven-tier cake?' groaned Blade, who hadn't actually wanted to make a cake in the first place. He had wanted to get giant banana leaves and go parasailing across the pond. But as he had got to choose the last present (the awesome dragonfly ride), it was Buttercup's turn to choose this time.

'Yes we do,' Buttercup replied in a singsong voice. 'Otherwise the cake won't represent all seven of the Flower Nymph Clans. We've only got Bluebell and Daisy left. It won't take long.'

'Promise?' said Blade, in a pleading tone.

'Yes, I promise,' said Buttercup. 'Now let's get on so that we can get out of here. This place gives me the creeps!'

The friends had sneaked into Brodick Castle through a small window. They had checked all round the walls hoping to find a way in, before they found this tiny window at the very top of the North Tower. All the windows were shut tight, apart from this little portal, barely the size of a chocolate bar, with its latch sitting just off the locked position.

Despite its size, the window was still way too heavy for the Flower Nymphs to open.

'It won't budge,' said Buttercup.

'I know what we need,' said Blade.

And he fluttered down towards the gardens below. A few moments later he reappeared, holding a twig in his hands.

'This is oak. It's super strong. Trust me, I use it for sword fighting!'

The pair wedged the twig into the bottom of the window to give them extra leverage.

'On the count of three. One, two, th—'.

Whoosh... the window flew open and the two Flower Nymphs went tumbling inside.

'Oh no,' screamed Buttercup, panicking as she bounced off the stone floor of the castle. She looked back up at the tiny window. Luckily the twig had jammed between the windowpane and the ledge.

'Thank goodness,' she sighed in relief. 'I thought we were trapped in here!'

The two Flower Nymphs fluttered down through the castle corridors towards the second floor. Brodick Castle oozed with grandeur. The corridor walls were draped with large tapestries full of images of witches.

The White Witches smiled down at them fondly and waved as the Flower Nymphs fluttered past. In total contrast, the Night Witches growled and hissed and tried to lunge out of the tapestries to grab at them with their long, black fingers. To their utter disgust and frustration, all the Night Witches managed to achieve was to ruffle their own tapestries.

The corridors were illuminated by candlelight from magnificent chandeliers filled with white church candles that didn't seem to burn down. The candles were all exactly the same length and twinkled on and off in unison, as if being led by an invisible conductor.

As they fluttered along the corridors they passed numerous rooms.

Buttercup asked, 'Have you noticed that all the rooms have a different colour theme?'

'Huh!' replied Blade, who was still busy pretend fencing with the Night Witches in the tapestries.

'Look!' said Buttercup as she spun him around in mid-air, pointing into the room opposite.

The room was completely white. Instead of wallpaper, white silk sheets floated against the walls. The only piece of decoration was a white polar bear, lying on the floor in place of a rug. The bear's black claws and eyes stood out against the pure white backdrop of the room like spilled oil glistening on a blanket of snow.

'Come on,' said Buttercup. 'He looks scary.'

'It's just a rug,' shrugged Blade and he fluttered into the room. As he did so, the bear closed his left eye and winked at him. Blade gave the bear a cheeky wink back and continued fluttering towards him. The bear smiled, revealing a double row of serrated black teeth. Blade promptly turned round and fluttered straight back out the door.

'OK, OK let's go!' he said and increased the pace considerably.

They zoomed past dozens of rooms, all with closed doors. The next room they came across with the door open was bright red. There were no windows or chandeliers, but it was still really bright inside.

Buttercup stopped to have a look.

'What are you doing,' hollered Blade. He grabbed Buttercup back out of the room.

'I don't actually know,' said Buttercup shaking her head. 'I just had an overwhelming urge to go inside!'

The room had a red fluid dripping down the walls. At first glance, they thought it was tears, as though the room was weeping. But as they were drawn closer, they could see it was much more viscous than tears. It looked more like blood, running down the walls and flowing into the middle of the room, then down a funnel right in the centre.

Before they realised it, they were both inside the room. Buttercup drifted towards the funnel, hypnotised by the flowing sea of red. Blade was also swaying towards the centre of the room, but with a little more resistance than Buttercup. A drip of red fluid fell onto one of his wings and he suddenly snapped out of his trance. He grabbed onto Buttercup's arm and fluttered as fast as his eight tiny wings could carry him out of the room, Buttercup in tow.

'That was a beautiful room, wasn't it?' she murmured, still under the room's spell.

'Yes, wonderful,' replied Blade rolling his eyes in the back of his head. 'I think it would improve our chances of survival considerably if we don't go into any more rooms,' he dictated.

'OK then,' replied Buttercup, still not quite with it.

They fluttered down one more flight of stairs and all the way along another corridor. This corridor was different from all of the others. There were no tapestries or chandeliers and only one door, at the very end.

The door was closed. A bright yellow light beamed out through the keyhole, so strong that it lit up the entire corridor with a yellowish shimmer.

The door was solid, so they decided to slide in through the keyhole.

'Ladies first,' sniggered Blade, bowing his head and leading Buttercup to the keyhole with his arm.

'Really?' said Buttercup raising her voice. 'You've never acted like a gentleman before. Why all of a sudden now? Let me guess… could it be because we're inside a spooky castle, and now we have to go into an even spookier room?'

Buttercup tucked her long, golden hair behind her ears, closed her eyes and popped her head through the keyhole. She then pulled her body through with her wings tightly shut behind her. When she was fully inside the room, she opened her eyes. It was breathtaking. Unlike the other rooms where she basically felt as though they were trying to eat her, this room felt warm and welcoming.

Also, unlike the others, this room was furnished. There was a little four-poster bed with a soft, lemon quilt spread over it that puddled onto the floor below.

The two arch-shaped windows had curtains made from yellow tulip petals pinned in an upside down 'V' and a big wooden trunk painted yellow, with the words 'Toy Box' carved into it, sat in one corner.

'Ouch,' yelped Buttercup as Blade came hurtling through the keyhole and charged straight into her back.

'This is a child's room,' he announced, hovering in the air with his hands on his waist, feeling rather pleased with himself that he'd actually made it through the keyhole.

'Well done, Sherlock,' snapped Buttercup.

'I've heard the rumours about this room, but I didn't believe them!' Blade said.

'I knew all along that the stories were true,' said Buttercup. 'My mum told me she was here when she was a little girl and that she'd met "the child". That's how I found out about the house.'

She pointed over to the other corner of the room,

where there stood the most fabulous dolls' house. It was five stories high, with seven bedrooms, three bathrooms, a lounge and a fully fitted kitchen, complete with working oven.

'It's just a dolls' house,' said Blade, unimpressed.

'It's a dolls' house with an *oven*,' Buttercup retorted. 'The only oven this size on the whole of the island. And we need it to bake Lily's birthday cake!'

Buttercup and Blade set to work baking the cake inside the little kitchen.

Despite the oven's tiny size, it was still really difficult for them to open and close the door. They pushed together to open the door for cake layer number six to go in.

'What was that?' gasped Buttercup, nearly jumping out of her skin... again! Every time she heard a noise she would spring up and start scanning the room.

'It's only the wind blowing against the curtains,' said Blade, rather unconvincingly. He too was feeling very jittery. They had both heard the stories about what happened inside the castle when the sun set.

The castle had once been home to Mogdred, the dark Night Witch. After her battle with Lizzie the Protector, she had become vulnerable and fled her lair for fear of being captured by the coven. But, in her haste to escape, she left something behind. Something so evil, that even Mogdred herself was afraid of it. Something that only came out after dark!

'Oh, dragonfly droppings,' said Buttercup. 'We're all out of pollen flour.'

'Aw, that's too bad,' smirked Blade. 'Looks like we'll have to settle for a six-tier cake!'

'Under no circumstances can we leave out one of the

Flower Nymph clans,' insisted Buttercup. 'You know what we're like. It would be war! I'll go and get some more pollen flour and you can decorate the sixth layer of the cake when it comes out of the oven.'

'Not on your shiny yellow chinny chin, chin,' replied Blade. '*I'll* get the pollen flour and *you* can decorate the cake, all alone here in Creepy McCreepsville!'

'Oh for goodness sake,' snapped Buttercup. 'Fine... you get the pollen flour. But don't dawdle. It's getting late and we want to be well out of here before the sun sets.'

Blade flew through the keyhole and along the corridor at the speed of light. The air in the corridor felt colder than when they'd arrived and the pimples on his body were beginning to throb. He flew up the staircase, back towards the North Tower. When he reached the top of the stairs he turned left.

'I'm sure it's left,' he thought. 'Or was it right? Oh sugarsnaps – it was right.'

He spun round and fluttered back in the opposite direction. After a few seconds, he stopped in his tracks. His wings were still fluttering, but he wasn't going anywhere!

He started to feel a tightening sensation around his left ankle. He looked down to see a thick, dark green rope twisting around his leg and up towards his knee, at which point he realised it wasn't a rope at all: it was creeping ivy, pulling him back along the corridor towards a newly opened door.

Blade's entire body went poker stiff. Then he arched backwards and howled like a werewolf as his thorns started to push through his skin. Every pimple wept with sap as the razor-sharp thorns penetrated his delicate skin.

45

They emerged from his body, transforming Blade into a prickly green porcupine. The thorns slashed through the ivy as though they were cutting candyfloss. The severed ropes of ivy fell to the ground, writhing around trying to find their prey.

Blade's wings had now all but disappeared under his thorny spines. He too fell to the ground, then sprang to his feet and ran along the corridor, slashing through the creeping ivy as it tried to encoil him.

As he ran past the open door to the Green Room, Blade glanced in for a split second. Dozens of long fingers of creeping ivy came whooshing out towards him, grasping at his spiky body. Inside the room there was a multitude of giant venus fly traps with their jaws wide open, poised to eat him!

He kept running as fast as he could. The muscles in his legs were on fire. He wasn't used to using them much and they felt as though they were about to collapse at any moment.

He could see the tiny open window up ahead, but the long arm of ivy was right behind him. The arm just kept regrowing new hands and fingers every time he slashed through them!

He knew he'd need to fly up to the window, but if he retracted his thorns the ivy would capture him!

He was just centimetres from the window when he stopped running and started spinning on the spot. Faster and faster he spun, ripping through the ivy's freshly formed hands and fingers. After a minute, the ivy withdrew its long arm to repair itself. Blade immediately retracted his thorns and flew straight up and out of the window, still spinning as he went.

*Blade*

'I'm free,' he yelled, as he twirled towards the ground in a celebratory spin. 'Free I tell you,' he laughed back up towards the ivy.

'*Arrghh*,' he shouted and threw his hands up in the air to stop the speeding oak twig from smashing him in the face. It came thrashing down, missing him by just a few millimetres.

'Oh no!' he squealed and shot through the air, back up to the little window at the top of the North Tower. It was now firmly closed with the latch locked tight.

## Chapter 6

## *Tweezel Berries*

'Great, the sun is just setting,' said Thumble Tumble. 'The tweezel berry bushes usually come out about now.'

Jock and Thumble Tumble flew down to the ground in front of a mass of dark green bushes that were at least three metres tall, and stretched along as far as they could see.

Thumble Tumble hopped off her broom and tapped it three times with her wand. The broom stood to attention, then bowed all the way to the ground, folding itself in half. It then halved again two more times, down to the size of a small comb, and popped itself inside the long pocket at the front of Thumble Tumble's dress.

'How do we get in?' asked Jock, a rather daunted expression on his face. The never-ending sea of green foliage didn't so much as have a slit in it, let alone an entrance!

'The entrance to the maze is supposed to just appear for people who really need something!' said Thumble Tumble, also looking quite dismayed at the size of the impenetrable green wall. 'That's how Minx got in! He needed to get lost, and so he found Devil's Maze! That's it,' she continued excitedly. 'We *need* to find tweezel berries. All we have to do is concentrate really hard about finding them and the maze will let us in!'

'That sounds easy enough. But, how do we get out again if we can't fly?' said Jock, looking anxious.

'That's a wee bit trickier,' said Thumble Tumble. 'Why don't we worry about that after we've found the tweezel berries?'

'Er, I'd love to, but I'm *already* worrying.' Jock's forehead now resembled a piece of lined paper, he was frowning so much.

'Look, all we need to do is use a shrinking spell to make us just a few centimetres tall and then use the mouseholes,' said Thumble Tumble, trying to sound confident, as though the plan wasn't quite as tricky as she'd made it sound.

Rather than reassuring Jock, this made him even more anxious than ever. Huge beads of sweat started rolling down his forehead and into his eyes.

He had good reason to be nervous. He could still remember the last time Thumble Tumble used her shrinking spell on him! They had been playing near the lily pond and he had happened to wonder what it would be like to float across the pond on a lily pad.

'No problem,' Thumble Tumble had piped up, raising her ever so slightly crooked wand above her head.

'REDUCIO!' she said, whereupon silver sparks flew out of the tip of her wand.

'It's working!' she cried. 'You'll soon be the size of a tiny bumble bee!'

The sparks showered Jock's head with a spray of tiny silver stars. He started to feel his jaws tighten and his teeth began aching. He could feel the skin around his eyes pulling backwards towards his ears, which were popping constantly.

He was feeling dizzy and nauseous. He could hear a strange noise, like air being let out of a balloon. The noise stopped and at the same time, so did the pain in his head, which was now the size of a bumble bee!

Unfortunately, his body was still the size of a dragon's, and he had to walk around for an entire week being referred to as 'pin-head', until the spell finally wore off.

'I know the spell went a little bit wonky the last time. But I've been practising loads. Let me show you,' said Thumble Tumble as she rummaged in her dress pocket to find her wand.

'No, no, it's fine,' Jock said quickly, thinking it would be better to have his full-size head if he was going to have to venture into Devil's Maze.

'OK, let's concentrate,' said Thumble Tumble in a determined voice. She closed her eyes and started to imagine Lily's face lighting up when she handed her a big jug of tweezel berry juice at her birthday party.

Jock wasn't on quite the same wavelength as Thumble Tumble. As soon as he closed his eyes, he imagined he was being tied to the ground by dozens of little men dressed in grass skirts, who started dancing around him in a circle and chanting in a strange language. They all had bare feet and a huge bone through their noses. Some of them were wearing necklaces. Jock strained his eyes to see what was on the necklaces, but the men were too far away.

A man wearing a large necklace began to walk towards

Jock. He was holding a vial in his hands that had a green smoke bellowing from it.

'Yunga marta bay?'

The little figure seemed to be asking him a question.

He walked closer to Jock, repeating the same words over and over – 'Yunga marta bay?'

He stood right above Jock's head, which was now pinned to the ground by twenty vine ropes hammered in with pegs carved from dwarf teeth.

The little man looked straight into Jock's left eye. (Jock's right eye was flat against the dirt, with his head angled on its side from the way he was tied down.)

'Yunga marta bay?' the little creature screeched at the top of his lungs, exposing his pointy teeth.

Jock didn't reply. He could now see the charms attached to the man's necklace – four shrunken heads, no doubt of previous victims. Jock was convinced he was to be number five.

The little creature pulled a long thin blade from his waistband and held it high above his head.

'Do you think it's this way?' Thumble Tumble's voice came booming into Jock's head.

He opened his eyes and let out a huge sigh of relief as he saw Thumble Tumble pointing her long thin wand towards an opening in the bushes.

'Have you been daydreaming about Head Shrinking Pixies again?' asked Thumble Tumble.

'Come on. We've got no time to play with pixies just now. We need to find tweezel berries,' she hollered and marched straight through the opening and into the maze.

Jock wasn't looking forward to the hunt for tweezel berry bushes. He dragged his long tail through the opening.

The second the tip of his tail was through, the bushes closed over, leaving them stuck, inside Devil's Maze.

'We should split up,' said Thumble Tumble, very excited to be inside the maze. 'As soon as one of us spots a tweezel berry bush, we'll shout out.'

Mm, I think it would be a better idea if we stick together,' replied Jock. 'They can be slippery characters and it will probably take both of us to catch one!'

Jock had no intention of splitting up. He was still spooked from his close shave with the Head Shrinking Pixies... daydream or not!

'Oh, alright then,' groaned Thumble Tumble. 'Let's try this way,' and she headed off along a narrow dirt path with tall green bushes on either side. The bushes were all identical, making it impossible for them to work out where they were.

They had only been walking for a few minutes, when a man appeared out of nowhere, running towards them, waving his hands in the air and screaming, 'They're alive... the bushes are alive. I need to get out of here!'

Willie had been on his way home from work. He was already late and it was taking ages for him to walk around the outer edge of the maze.

'I'm going to be late for dinner,' he had groaned to himself. 'I really need to find a shortcut.'

As soon as the word 'cut' left his mouth, he was standing inside the maze.

'What's going on?' he thought.

'Hello! Hello! Is there anyone there?' he shouted out.

Not a sound.

Willie started walking along the path. He was sure he could hear footsteps behind him.

'Hello!' he said, and turned round to greet whoever it was.

There was nothing there, other than a tall bush standing right in the middle of the path. The bush had bright yellow leaves and purple berries hanging from its branches.

'That's strange,' Willie thought, then turned around and continued on his journey home. A few seconds later he heard the footsteps again. He spun round to find the same bush standing right behind him.

This time he glanced down to the base of the bush. It had branches sticking out at the bottom that looked a bit like two bony feet with long toes.

As he hurriedly turned to carry on along the path, Willie saw the bush tiptoe towards him out of the corner of his eye.

'Yikes,' he thought, 'I'm not imagining this. This thing's alive!'

He turned on his heels and ran as fast as he could, screaming at the top of his voice, 'I need to get out of here.'

And that's when he ran straight past Thumble Tumble and Jock.

Suddenly, an opening appeared in the maze wall right in front of Willie and he ran straight through it. The maze closed instantly behind him.

'I think he needed a way out,' laughed Thumble Tumble. 'Come on, let's get the tweezel berry bush that spooked him.'

And she ran along the path in the direction Willie had come from.

The tweezel berry bush was no longer tiptoeing. It was now sprinting away from them like an Olympic runner.

Despite its speed, Thumble Tumble was gaining on it. Soon she was only inches away. The bush took a sharp left. Thumble Tumble swung left behind it and pounced with both hands out in front of her.

'Gotcha,' she yelled, and fell, face-first, onto the dirt path.

Jock came pounding round the corner right behind her.

'Watch out,' she shouted up, just as she saw Jock leap over her.

He landed with a thunderous thud that sent tremors all through the maze.

'That was close,' he panted.

'I know,' said Thumble Tumble, scrambling to her feet. 'We nearly had it.'

She raced off along the path.

'You go straight and I'll keep going left,' she hollered back towards Jock.

Jock was about to head off, when he paused. He could hear something in the bushes beside him. It was very quiet, like someone tiptoeing! He walked slowly along the path, listening intently. The sound was getting louder. He stopped just before a turn in the path and listened. He could definitely hear scraping noises. He dived around the corner and charged like a bull.

'Oh no!' he shouted, slamming his feet hard into the dirt as he went skidding along the ground. He swung sideways and his huge tail banged into the bushes, slowing him down even more… but it wasn't enough!

Blade had just managed to pick himself up off the ground after being thrown down by the shockwaves from Jock's earthshattering thud.

He was still trying to wipe the dirt out of his eyes when he saw the wall of purple scales coming crashing towards him. He turned to run, but tripped over a twig and fell back onto the dirt path. He tried to pull himself up as the mass of purple screeched closer. It was too late. Blade closed his eyes.

CRASH!

The two bodies collided together and rolled along the path like a giant tyre, before falling to the ground.

Blade opened his eyes and ran towards the crash site. Jock was sitting up. He was a little dazed, but otherwise he was completely unscathed.

Thumble Tumble was lying, lifeless, on the path. Her little body was as flat as a pancake. Every bone had been crushed by Jock steamrollering over her.

'We need help,' Blade shouted as loud as he could.

Within an instant, a tweezel berry bush appeared from the maze walls. It gently slipped Thumble Tumble's body across its right foot and began gliding along through the maze.

Jock dragged himself to his feet.

'Are you OK?' gasped Blade.

'I'm fine. How's Thumble Tumble?' he replied in a sluggish tone.

'I don't know,' said Blade shaking his head. 'But it's not looking good. We really need to get her home. Her aunts will know what to do.'

Within a few minutes, they were back at the entrance to the maze. The dark green bushes parted like curtains opening at the theatre and the tweezel berry bush slid Thumble Tumble's flat little body gently onto the ground. It then floated back into the maze and disappeared as the wall of bushes re-formed, like a giant jigsaw putting itself together.

Jock lay Thumble Tumble's body on his wing and Blade gathered up some long grass to tie her on. He twisted the grass around her body then tied it in a knot at the ends.

'That's secure,' he said. 'Are you sure you're OK to fly?'

'Yes, I'm fine,' said Jock sadly. 'But she's not. Let's go.'

He spread out his huge wings and soared high up into the sky. Blade followed close behind.

## Chapter 7

## *Body Pumps*

Isla was in the kitchen, cooking up a batch of her favourite jam, Everfruit. She had already added apples, strawberries, tweezel berries, pineapple and brambles, and was now deciding whether to add some rambutan.

The good thing about Everfruit jam is that you can add as many different fruits as you want, and it always tastes amazing. As she walked over to the cupboard to get the rambutan, Isla felt the hairs on the back of neck stand up as a waft of cold air swept through the cottage.

On the final approach to the cottage, Blade had broken away and flown straight towards the door like a speeding bullet. He knew the door was enchanted and that it would open automatically for a White Witch.

'Watch out,' hollered Jock. 'You need to slow down.'

But Blade didn't pay him any attention. By the time he realised the door wasn't opening, it was too late! He twirled in the air and smashed into it backwards. His wings crushed into his back as he slid down the door.

'This door only opens automatically for witches who

are conscious,' said Jock, landing gently beside him.

'Oh?' groaned Blade.

Jock untied Thumble Tumble's body and placed her hand against the door. Instantly, the glass porthole in the centre opened like a kaleidoscope. The entire door then evaporated into the frame, leaving fresh air where the solid door had been.

'What has happened?' Isla cried.

'I'm so sorry,' said Jock, tears rolling down his cheeks. 'I crushed her… It was an accident. I just couldn't stop!'

'Take a deep breath and tell me what happened,' said Isla as she knelt down beside Thumble Tumble's body.

Jock's voice was trembling as he spoke.

'I thought I heard a tweezel berry bush tiptoeing through the maze. But it wasn't a tweezel berry bush, it was Thumble Tumble and I just couldn't stop in time.' He started sobbing loudly. 'I'm so sorry!' he said.

'Was she facing you?' asked Isla calmly.

She leaned closer over Thumble Tumble's body.

'Yes. Yes she was,' gulped Jock.

He couldn't get the look of terror on Thumble Tumble's face out of his mind. 'She must have been so afraid when she saw me hurtling towards her,' he thought.

'Did she have her wand?' Isla continued quizzing him.

'YES, she had her wand,' he cried out. 'But it was too late. I crushed her before she had a chance to use it. It was horrible. Please stop asking me about it. Please? I can't bear to think about it anymore.'

'I need to know exactly what happened, Jock,' Isla said firmly.

'I killed her! That's what happened. Are you satisfied now?'

Jock stood up to his full height, shaking his head angrily.

His eyes were bulging out of his head. They had turned bright red from the bloodshot veins caused by his tears. He didn't look like Jock anymore. He resembled a fierce beast of a dragon as he towered above Isla.

Isla stared straight up into his eyes. She had never been afraid of Jock before and she wasn't going to start being afraid of him now.

'Calm down, Jock,' she said gently. 'I need to know this, it's important. Did you see her do anything at all before you collided?'

Jock closed his eyes and tried to visualise the accident in his head. There was nothing. All he had seen was the cloud of dust from the path as they collided.

'Well?' pressed Isla.

'No, nothing! I couldn't see anything because of the dust,' Jock wailed.

'I need you to concentrate, Jock. What colour was the dust?' Isla continued.

'It was grey. No, it was actually more like green. Greeny-grey. That was it,' he mumbled.

'I knew it,' Isla exclaimed triumphantly. 'Thumble Tumble used a paper spell. No offence Jock, but I knew she wouldn't just let you *crush* her!'

Isla took the wand out of the pocket in her oversized purple dress and pointed it at Thumble Tumble's head.

'PUMPSOMATICO!'

A stream of tiny orange drops flowed out from the end of her wand and surrounded Thumble Tumble's wafer-thin body.

After a few seconds, the orange drops started to change

shape and morphed into little bicycle pumps, each with a
needle-like snout and a hand attached to the top. There
was no arm or body, just a brown hairy hand holding onto
each little pump.

The pumps then began stabbing their sharp snouts into
Thumble Tumble. They pierced her arms, legs, tummy
and face.

When all of the pumps were attached, Isla raised her
wand again.

'REINFLATIUM!'

Each hand clenched tightly around their pump's handle
and they all began to move up and down simultaneously.
Thumble Tumble's legs, arms, tummy and face started
to plump up. Slowly but surely, her entire body began to
inflate like a bouncy castle.

The first parts of her body to pop back were her feet.
These were followed by her legs, tummy and arms. Lastly,
her face started to move like a contortionist's. It stretched
sideways, pulling her lips right to the end of her cheeks.
Then it elongated in a vertical line, before finally popping
back into shape. Thumble Tumble's body kept inflating.
Her tummy was like a balloon getting bigger and bigger.
Eventually, she started to float up into the air.

'Halt!' Isla shouted.

At that, the pumps immediately disengaged. Isla raised
her wand and whispered:

'DEFLATIUM MINIMUM.'

A small drizzle of air expelled from Thumble Tumble.
It was a most repulsive sound. The horrible wheezing
lasted for about ten seconds and then Thumble Tumble's
body was back to normal. She looked as though she was
just lying on the floor fast asleep.

Isla walked over to the kitchen sink and turned on the tap. She put her hand in the water to check the temperature. When it was just above freezing, she waved her hand and a large black cauldron floated across the kitchen and positioned itself under the tap. When it was full, Isla turned off the tap. She put the tip of her finger onto the lip of the cauldron and raised her arm. The cauldron lifted up into the air and followed Isla back over to where Thumble Tumble was lying. Isla took her finger away and the cauldron remained suspended in the air above Thumble Tumble's body. Isla gently tipped the cauldron and emptied the water all over Thumble Tumble.

'*Argh...* what did you do that for?' Thumble Tumble screamed, jumping up off of the wet floor. 'You could have clapped your hands in my ear or used smelling salts instead!'

Isla couldn't help laughing.

'I know,' she said. 'But this was way much more fun!'

'For who?' stormed Thumble Tumble.

'Why, for me of course,' snorted Isla, as she waved her hand again to dry up the wet floor. 'Now, can you lot explain to me exactly *what* you were doing inside Devil's Maze?'

'Oh, well er, you see...' squirmed Thumble Tumble. 'We needed to get a cool present for Lily, so we decided to get some tweezel berries from the maze.'

'*We*,' thought Jock. 'More like *you*!'

'Really?' said Isla, raising her voice for the first time since they had returned home. 'Do you know how dangerous the maze is?'

Isla was about to launch into one of her rants, when she was cut off by Blade.

'Isla's right,' he interjected. 'Devil's Maze can be really dodgy. You shouldn't go back in there *ever again,* in case you end up leaving your friend behind, inside the castle for the Mantigh to find!'

Blade's eyes welled up with tears as he spoke.

'Oh my goodness, Blade, why didn't you say something sooner?' asked Isla, trying to wipe away his tears. But instead, she practically knocked his head off with her stubby fingers. Blade went flying backwards and splatted against Thumble Tumble's nose.

Thumble Tumble peeled Blade off of her nose and stood him in the palm of her hand.

'I forgot,' he said in a whisper, lowering his head. 'I was on my way to get help when I saw Jock crush Thumble Tumble, and it just went straight out of my mind.' He shook his tiny head and continued to stare straight down into Thumble Tumble's palm. 'What kind of friend am I?' he mumbled. 'Buttercup is trapped inside Brodick Castle at night and I *forget* about her!'

'Oh, that isn't good,' said Isla. 'It's already past eight o'clock and the sun will be setting soon. There's no way you can go back into the castle tonight.'

Blade gave Isla a defiant stare, but he knew she was right. There was no way back into the castle.

'You three stay here. I'm going to find Bessie,' Isla said, and clicked her fingers in the air.

A thin stream of orange glitter dust wound its way from the tip of her finger to the door handle on the cupboard under the stairs. It coiled around the handle like a snake, turning it in a clockwise direction.

Inside the cupboard there was a row of six pegs. Hooded cloaks hung from three of them.

One cloak was slightly shorter than the others. It was bright red and looked almost new. The other cloaks were much older.

One was deep purple and made from silk. It had patches all over where it had been repaired, and a giant cobweb spun all the way from the hood to the hem, with a rather nasty looking spider sitting right in the middle, scowling at them.

The third cloak was also quite tatty looking. It was brown and green with bits of moss and leaves clinging to it.

A broom was hanging from three of the other pegs. These pegs had a little wooden plaque above them with a name carved into it. The first was 'Bessie', the second 'Isla' and the third 'Lizzie'.

The beam of orange dust swirled past the horrid looking spider and around the green cloak, unhooking it from the peg and carrying it over to Isla. She slipped it on and reached into the cupboard to get her broom.

The broom was old and grubby, just like her cloak. Its wooden handle had numerous notches gouged out of it and there was a chink about three-quarters of the way along that would make it almost impossible to fly in a straight line. The head was made from feathers – not very traditional for a witch's broom, but Isla found it useful when cleaning!

She headed towards the front door, which disappeared on her approach from the porthole outwards.

At the entrance, Isla turned to Thumble Tumble and said sternly, 'Do not leave the house.' She then hitched up her cloak and sat on her broom side-saddle.

As soon as her bottom touched the broom, it went

zooming through the doorway, so fast that she almost fell off. She grabbed tight with both hands and soared up into the sky, her feet dangling out behind her.

Within a few seconds, Isla was gone and the solid door started to re-emerge from its frame.

The door had almost completely rematerialised with only the porthole to move back into position when it suddenly stopped, leaving a gaping hole in the centre.

Thumble Tumble was standing just a few feet from the doorway with her hand stretched out.

'We *can't* leave Buttercup alone in Brodick Castle,' she said defiantly to Jock and Blade.

And she marched towards the open doorway.

## Chapter 8

## *Dead Souls Waking*

Buttercup could see through the window that the sun was beginning to set. The bright yellow room was gathering shadows as the light faded.

The air temperature had started to drop, and the warm, sun-kissed air was replaced by a gloomy, stale atmosphere.

Shadows stretched from wall to wall as the sun disappeared below the horizon. Buttercup stared, mesmerised, as the shadows formed different shapes on the wall. She could see three triangles and four circles, one large and three small. The shapes were dancing around, creating an array of patterns.

Buttercup watched as the shadows formed themselves into the image of a boy's face. The big circle was his head, the little circles his eyes and nose, and the triangles his spiky hair. The cheery, round-faced boy smiled down at Buttercup, then he started to melt. The triangles of hair dripped down the wall, dragging the eyes and nose with them. The triangles stopped just where the boy's smile had been and flipped upside-down to create a frightening monster with drooping eyes and pointed teeth.

Buttercup launched up from the floor and fluttered as fast as she could out of the dolls' house kitchen and into the living room, where two tiny toy lamps still glowed on a table. The dim light they gave was just enough to keep the shadows away.

As soon as she fluttered into the living room, she heard a loud bang from outside the dolls' house.

She dived behind a toy settee, which still had two dolls perched on it ready for playing at afternoon tea.

Buttercup's heart was pounding. It was so loud inside her head she could barely hear. She strained her ears and listened intently for any more sounds, but there was nothing.

After ten minutes of playing solitary statues, Buttercup crept sideways and edged her head around the arm of the settee. She let out a gentle sigh at the sight of the rolling pin she had been using earlier rocking back and forth on the tiled floor.

'It must have rolled off the table,' she thought, and she began to stand up.

There was another huge thud. She looked out from the dolls' house to see the toy box in the corner of the yellow room fly open.

The lid of the toy box shot straight up into the air and hit off the ceiling, before catapulting around the room. It smashed into a wall, then catapulted back and sliced through the top of the dolls' house, taking the entire top floor with it, before crashing to the ground. The lid exploded into tiny pieces which scattered everywhere. The force of the explosion threw Buttercup halfway across the little living room inside the dolls' house.

With the entire roof gone, she was completely exposed. She scrambled to her feet and ran towards the lamp table. She could hear screams reverberating from the toy box. She threw herself onto the wooden floor with her hands out in front of her and slid underneath the table.

Her feet had barely disappeared under the table when three streams of grey smoke floated up out of the toy box. Two of the smoke strands were thick and dark and they were drifting either side of the third strand, which was much thinner and paler.

The two thick strands of smoke drifted out to the sides of the room, then began moving around in opposite directions. One was circling clockwise at floor level and the other was gliding just below the ceiling.

Buttercup placed her hands over her ears to try to shut out the shrieks as she watched the strands of smoke spin around the room. She was so dizzy from watching the spinning smoke that she started to feel sick. She pulled her hands away from her ears and held them tightly across her mouth. She could feel a burning sensation in her throat.

'*No*. Please don't throw up... not now!' she thought.

She could feel the hot liquid inside her mouth trying to escape through the gaps between her fingers. The first drips of vomit fell to the floor. Buttercup watched as the droplets fell in slow motion. They landed on the floor one at a time. In her mind, it sounded like a drum-roll.

'Oh no,' Buttercup thought, as another swell of hot liquid moved up into her mouth. The burning sensation was unbearable. She crouched down and took her hands away from her mouth.

At the very same moment the swirling smoke strands stopped their dizzying movement and the one at floor level fell to the ground, leaving a circle of ash.

Buttercup felt hugely relieved as the sick feeling inside her instantly subsided.

The ash from the circle started shifting in towards the centre of the room, rising up as it moved to form the silhouette of a creature with a crooked nose and hairs sticking out from her pointy chin.

Buttercup had heard stories about these creatures, but she hadn't believed them. She thought they were just old wives' tales made up to scare children so they wouldn't go into Brodick Castle at night.

She lay still on the floor and watched as the second strand of smoke performed the same ritual, forming into an equally foul-looking witch.

The two witches walked over to the toy box and called out in unison, 'Silusa, where are you? Come out, come out, wherever you are. It's time to play!'

The light grey stream of smoke started to turn in the air. It spiralled away from the toy box and hurtled around like a mini-tornado, leaving destruction in its wake. It passed over the bed pulling the lemon quilt off with one twist. The quilt flew against the window, ripping the tulip-petal curtains in half.

The mini-tornado then changed direction. It was coming towards the dolls' house, where Buttercup was lying under the table, terrified.

'Pull yourself together,' she shouted to herself inside her head.

It worked. A split second before the tornado struck she grabbed hold of the table legs. She lifted her body up off the floor and fluttered as hard as she could in reverse.

The tornado grabbed at the table legs as though it

*Mantigh*

was trying to rip a tree out by its roots. Buttercup closed her eyes and gripped with all her might. The tornado passed in just a few seconds. Buttercup opened her eyes to the delightful vision of the underside of the table still shielding her tiny body.

She lay back down on the floor with her chin on the ground and looked on in silence as the mini-tornado came to a halt right in front of her nose. The particles of ash fused together into a grey sphere which rose up into the air then dropped and bounced off the floor, where it exploded, revealing the third witch. This witch was much smaller than the other two. She didn't have a crooked nose or a pointed chin. In fact, she looked almost human, apart from her body being made from dust and ash, rather than flesh and skin!

Buttercup's childhood nightmares had just become reality. The creatures were Mantigh – witches' souls!

Neither dead nor alive, they just existed. They would slumber through the daylight hours and set out after sunset on their nightly hunt.

Their prey? Any living thing, for the Mantigh fed on life force.

As a child, Buttercup had heard many versions of the chilling Mantigh stories. The tales had kept her awake at night. She remembered how she would lie with her blanket pulled up to her chin, eyes wide open, staring at the ceiling of her bedroom, terrified.

Squeezing her eyes tight shut, she tried to remember the stories her mum had told her about the evil Night Witch, Mogdred and her half-sister, Silusa.

Mogdred despised Silusa because she was not a 'true' Night Witch. Their father was a dark warlock, but Silusa's mother was a White Witch. And her mother's goodness was stronger than the dark magic of her father, making Silusa, loving and kind.

After the death of her mother, Mogdred imprisoned Silusa in her bedroom (a beautifully enchanting room that was decorated in her favourite colour... yellow).

Mogdred's thirst for power led her deeper and deeper into dark magic. And so, when she heard of a cauldron that could bring the dead back to life, she had to have it! The Cauldron of Undry was considered to be so dangerous that the Council of Witches had it sent to the Holy Isle, where it was hidden by the Buddhists to make sure it could never fall into the wrong hands.

Mogdred knew the Buddhists would never surrender the cauldron to her, so she sent Silusa to meet with them. The Buddhists could see that Silusa's heart was pure and so they revealed the cauldron to her. When its whereabouts were revealed, Mogdred attacked the temple to take the cauldron by force. During the battle, Mogdred fired a death bolt that, instead of hitting a Buddhist, struck Silusa in the heart.

Mogdred and her army fled the Holy Isle with Silusa's body and the cauldron. When they returned to her castle, Mogdred used the power of the cauldron to bring Silusa back to life. But it was not Silusa who returned from the dead. The creature that awoke that night was pure evil: it was a Mantigh.

As soon as it opened its eyes, it threw its arms out either side and grabbed the two Night Witches who had been standing over Silusa's body. The creature held on to the two witches, clenching tightly, until it had drained every drop of life from them.

Mogdred used the cauldron once again on the two dead Night Witches, but after she used it for the third time, the cauldron evaporated into thin air and disappeared back to the safety of the Buddhists.

The Mantigh she had created were so evil, that Mogdred herself was afraid of what they might do. So she cast a powerful spell over the castle, preventing them from ever leaving. Well, at least until she could find a way to control them!

'Come on, let's play seek and eat!'

Buttercup's eyes shot open at the sound of the smallest Mantigh's haunting voice.

'Sounds like fun,' cackled the largest of the Mantigh as she put her hands by her sides and started to wriggle. As she wriggled, her body began to change shape. She became taller and thinner and her eyes and mouth closed and stretched out until they were just black slits. After a few more wriggles, her entire body transformed into a long grey snake. The head of the snake still resembled the witch's face, making it even more hideous.

'Come on then,' she hissed, and she flew up into the air and slithered off through the keyhole in the bedroom door.

The other large Mantigh had also started to wriggle with her hands by her sides. Her body transformed into an eel that swam through the air towards the keyhole, snapping its jaws, before disappearing to the other side.

The smallest Mantigh's body started to fade into ash. It had almost completely transformed, when suddenly, she came straight back into form.

'Come out, come out where ever you are,' she began to chant. 'I can f*eeee*l you.'

Buttercup held her breath.

The little Mantigh began floating around the room. She popped her head under the bed.

'Not here,' she sang.

She floated across the floor and up the wall, and slipped behind the curtains.

'Not here either!'

'I know you're here. I can *feeee*l you,' she taunted venomously as she floated over the derelict dolls' house.

She stopped right above it and took a deep breath, then grinned.

Buttercup was quaking with fear.

'I can *feeee*l you, I can *feeee*l you,' Silusa chanted as she floated right into the dolls' house.

Just then, a little white mouse darted out from the debris and scampered across the floor towards a tiny hole on the skirting board – and ran straight into Silusa's open mouth. She had floated under the floorboards and popped her head up right in front of the hole just as the mouse was running through it.

The mouse's whole body turned grey. As it did so, a flush of energy flowed through Silusa's body, turning her cheeks rosy pink and her hair as black as night. The wave of colour passed through her like an electric shock, then it was gone.

As the last flourish of colour faded from her cheeks, the lifeless body of the little mouse fell to the floor. Silusa then exploded in a puff of smoke that floated over to the door.

Just before she disappeared through the keyhole, the smoky image shot back into the room like a boomerang and whispered, 'I'll get you next time!'

## Chapter 9

## Number One Goatfell

'Hold on!' hollered Jock, grabbing Thumble Tumble's arm as she tried to march through the open doorway. 'We can't get into Brodick Castle after dark. The castle is sealed by powerful dark magic, so even spells won't work!'

There's got to be *something* we can do,' Thumble Tumble pleaded. 'We can't just leave Buttercup. The Mantigh will kill her.'

'She might be OK,' said Blade in a hopeful voice. 'When I left she was in the yellow room. The Mantigh are almost blind, so hopefully she'll be able to camouflage herself until morning.

'Oh no, that's the last place she wants to be!' said Jock.

'Why?' asked Blade, looking very concerned.

'That's Silusa's bedroom. It's where the Mantigh wake up!'

'What?' cried Blade 'The sun has set. She could be dead already!'

'Don't think like that, Blade,' said Thumble Tumble. 'The Mantigh can't see or hear very much. They feel your presence. It's life force they feel. Buttercup is so tiny they might not be able to feel her!'

'I just hope she remembers the stories about the Mantigh as well as you do,' said Blade, shaking his head. A single tear started to roll down the brave little nymph's cheek.

'We're not giving up hope yet,' said Jock. 'I think there might be someone who can help us.'

'Who?' asked Thumble Tumble.

'McCools,' he said. 'If anyone on this island knows how to get us into Brodick Castle, it's him!'

'We've no time to waste,' said Blade hastily. He fluttered a few inches off the ground, then fell, face-first, onto the floor. His wings were still crushed from his crash landing. The little nymph lay on the floor feeling helpless, looking up at Jock and Thumble Tumble.

'It's OK, Blade,' said Thumble Tumble. 'Besides, we need someone to stay here and let Isla and Bessie know where we've gone.'

Jock stepped through the doorway and spread out his huge wings, then flew up into the night sky. Thumble Tumble took her comb-size broom out of her pocket and tapped it gently. Within seconds, the broom was full size. She hopped on and flew up beside Jock.

When she had disappeared into the clouds, Blade stepped back inside the cottage and the magical door reappeared with the porthole back in place.

Jock was flying so fast that the wind from his wings almost threw Thumble Tumble off of her broom.

'Oi, wait up!' she hollered, and grabbed onto her broom with both hands.

'Sorry Thumble Tumble, but we need to get inside

Brodick Castle as fast as we can,' Jock shouted back over his shoulder. 'I didn't want to say anything in front of Blade, but I think Silusa *will* be able to feel Buttercup's presence. Because Silusa was once pure of heart, the Mantigh inside her body can feel those who are also pure of heart!'

'Even though she's so tiny?' asked Thumble Tumble, flying through the air as fast as she could possibly go. She was now neck and neck with Jock.

'Yes. We need to hurry! The only chance Buttercup has is if she hides. Silusa used to love to play games, especially hide and seek. If Buttercup hides, Silusa will play at seeking her through the night. But she *will* kill her, eventually. By sunrise, her thirst for life force will be so strong that she won't be able to stop herself!'

They had been flying for just over an hour when Jock said, 'We're here.' He threw his wings out in front of him and started flapping in reverse, then hovered on the spot like a helicopter silently sitting in the air. Slowing the pace of his wings, he began to descend towards the snow covered mountain below. His massive body drifted downwards like a feather in the breeze and gently landed on the edge of a cliff at the very top of the mountain.

'Be careful,' he shouted up to Thumble Tumble, who was already zooming in to land. 'This ledge isn't very…'

Before he could finish his sentence, Thumble Tumble landed hard and fast.

*Boom*! Down went her feet and as they hit the ground an enormous crack appeared right below her. The crack spread like a lightning fork, straight across the cliff edge, then the entire cliff detached itself from the mountain and started crashing towards the base, hundreds of feet below.

'Strong,' mumbled Jock through gritted teeth, with Thumble Tumble's cloak now firmly jammed between them. Thumble Tumble was dangling over the edge of the fallen cliff, grasping onto her cloak, which was now choking her like a noose around her neck – and gripping onto her broom with her other hand.

Jock swung his head around and dropped Thumble Tumble in a heap on the snow, right in front of a shiny red door. The door looked pretty strange. It didn't appear to be attached to a house, it was just standing by itself in the snow!

Thumble Tumble stood up and started to brush the snow off of her cloak and tights.

'It's freezing,' she said, her teeth chattering.

'Well, it does snow here for eleven and a half months of the year,' explained Jock. 'Knock the door then.'

He nodded at a big silver knocker in the centre of the door.

'Why?' asked Thumble Tumble. 'There's nothing behind it!'

'Look again,' said Jock.

Thumble Tumble rubbed her eyes to try to get the snow glare away and then walked a bit closer to the door. The snow around the door frame seemed a bit unusual. It wasn't glistening like the rest of the snow. She stared intently for a few seconds. Then, from out of the snow, she could see the silhouette of a house. A very tall, crooked house that was completely white... even the windows!

Thumble Tumble lifted the silver knocker and let it go. Not a peep! She lifted it again and this time she slammed it back against the silver back-plate, which had the number one carved into it. The knocker didn't make a sound. Thumble Tumble looked back at Jock as if to ask what to do next.

'Alright, alright,' McCools shouted from behind the door.

The noise from the knocker had vibrated along the hallway, which had shelves from floor to ceiling crammed with ornamental snails. The snails, in a variety of shapes, sizes and colours, were made from fragile materials, including glass, porcelain and crystal. The wave of noise from the door knocker had sent hundreds of ornamental snails crashing onto the marble floor below.

Leaving a rainbow of devastation in its wake, the noise vibration then burst through a big wooden door into the living room. This room was the polar opposite of the hallway. Here the walls were completely bare and unadorned. In front of the open fire stood a purple leather armchair and a little stool, on top of which was a half-full mug of cocoa and some crumbs of fruit cake on a plate. The vibration threw the mug onto the floor and spilled the cocoa over the cream rug. The cake crumbs blew onto the cocoa, decorating it like sprinkles on a cupcake.

McCools arrived at the front door just as the hurricane of noise was making its way upstairs. He turned the rusty, hexagon-shaped handle and pulled the door open. He could hear the books flying off of the book racks onto the floor in the library above him.

'Yes?' he yelled, straight into Thumble Tumble's face. 'Can I help you?'

Before she could catch her breath, McCools launched into a full-blown rant.

'Do you know how long it took me to collect those snails? *Do you*?' The fur on his body stuck out, making him look like an inflated pufferfish. '*Well*?' he snapped.

'Er... what snails?' asked Thumble Tumble sheepishly.

'Those snails!' McCools squealed, pointing at the floor.

Thumble Tumble was confused. All she could see was a mess of broken glass and pottery scattered all over the place.

'And I don't even want to begin to think about the library books,' McCools snorted, before slamming the door shut in Thumble Tumble's face.

A second later, the door reopened. McCools pushed straight past Thumble Tumble and swung his bony arms around Jock's leg. His spiky fur had softened back into a fluffy orange mass.

'What are you doing here? Are you in trouble? Is it Mogdred?' McCools babbled. Without giving Jock a chance to answer, he nodded towards Thumble Tumble. 'And who is that?' he asked.

'I'm not in trouble, but a friend of mine is,' Jock said.

'Friend?' McCools looked at Jock inquisitively. 'I didn't know you had any *friends*, Jock!'

'Yes, well, a lot changes in eight years,' said Jock.

'My goodness, has it been eight years?' asked McCools.

Thumble Tumble was still in shock after having a door slammed in her face. She was even more shocked when she realised that the little puff of orange rudeness was the infamous McCools!

Thumble Tumble had heard all about the super-intelligent, three-legged haggis. But apart from having three legs and being a haggis... this was not what she expected! She had imagined him being taller, with glasses – and a bit less orange! She also thought someone *that*

79

intelligent could not mistake a pile of rubble for a snail!

'And this is Thumble Tumble,' said Jock.

'Thumble what?'

'Thumble Tumble. You know, Lizzie's daughter.'

'Oh, so you're the new Protector,' said McCools. 'You don't look much like I imagined you would.'

'Ditto,' Thumble Tumble retorted.

'So how can I help you?' asked McCools.

'We need to get into Brodick Castle,' said Jock.

'Well that's simple... just wait until sunrise!' snorted McCools and he turned to head back indoors.

Thumble Tumble stepped in front of the door.

'It's not that simple,' she said. 'We need to get in now!'

'It's not humanly possible,' insisted McCools.

'*Not possible*! I thought you were supposed to be this super-brainy dude. You're just a fake!' said Thumble Tumble.

She stepped away from the door and with a condescending curtsy, waved McCools back into the house.

McCools frowned.

'I didn't say it's *not possible*. I said it's *not humanly possible*! For goodness sake, girl, clear your ears!'

Thumble Tumble turned bright pink. She didn't know if she was more embarrassed or angry at the rude comments emanating from this orange fur ball. She started twisting her wand in her fingers, feeling very tempted.

'And you may as well make some use of that spell you're conjuring up in your head,' said McCools. He had noticed Thumble Tumble's white knuckles and the fact that her face now resembled the colour of his door. 'Come on, we don't have all day!' he continued in the same sarcastic tone.

Thumble Tumble lifted her wand and pointed it straight at the back of McCools' head.

'Clear off!' she shouted, and a silver trail came shooting out of her wand. It went straight over the back of McCools' head, then spread out above the rubble like a blanket.

The broken ornaments lifted up off of the ground and stuck to the magic silver blanket. Within a flash, all of the broken ornaments were stuck to the blanket, which then rolled up and propped itself neatly in the corner of the hallway.

'Not too bad,' said McCools, with the tiniest hint of a smile. 'Look, there is only one way I know of to get into Brodick Castle after sunset. And it involves the use of dark magic… very dark.'

McCools had his most serious face on as he spoke, but even so, it was difficult for Jock and Thumble Tumble to take this fluffy orange ball seriously. They both looked away so that they wouldn't begin to laugh.

'Pay attention, you two!' McCools snapped, then he continued, almost in a whisper. 'There is a cauldron that contains the power to defeat the Mantigh. But the dark power within the cauldron is so dangerous, it was hidden by the Witch Council a long time ago to prevent it from ever falling into the wrong hands.'

'Where is it now?' asked Jock.

'I don't know,' said McCools, but I'm sure we'll find the answer in The Tome of Dark Discovery.'

'What is The Tome of Dark Discovery?' asked Thumble Tumble.

'It's a book that contains the whereabouts of every piece of dark magic in the world,' McCools explained.

81

'And it happens to be lying on the floor of my library upstairs… along with about another two thousand books! You'll need to wait here, Jock, unless this little lady can use a shrinking spell on you?'

No, no, I'll be fine here,' Jock said quickly.

As Thumble Tumble followed McCools along the hallway, it got lower and lower, and by the time they reached the end, the brim of her hat was skimming the ceiling.

Thumble Tumble had expected to arrive at a secret spiral staircase leading to the library. Instead, they were greeted with an old fashioned elevator that had an iron gate across the front. At the side of the gate there was a big round button with the letter H on it.

McCools pressed the button and the lift started to make its way down from the floor above. The elevator looked about a hundred years old and it sounded like a rusty old cart on a train track as it slowly descended. Five minutes passed before the gate finally opened.

'Wow!' said Thumble Tumble.

Her jaw fell open. The inside of the elevator was covered in emeralds. The floor, ceiling and walls were a mosaic of green shiny gems, with the exception of three ruby buttons on a little control panel. One had the letter H, the second had the letter T, and the third had the letters SE.

Thumble Tumble looked at the panel and frowned. 'If you don't mind me asking, can you tell me what SE stands for? I think H is hall and T is top, but I can't think of anything for SE!

'Not at all,' said McCools, and he pressed the ruby button with the letter T on it, then began to hum along with the music that was now streaming through the elevator.

'Well?' said Thumble Tumble. 'What does it mean?'

'Oh, I'm sorry,' said McCools. 'I thought you were asking if I don't mind you asking… and I don't.' He continued humming.

'Are you going to tell me?' snipped Thumble Tumble, folding her arms across her chest and tapping her left toe irritably on the ground.

'Oh, you like the music too? I find it very relaxing,' grinned McCools.

Thumble Tumble was anything but relaxed as she glared back at McCools. 'Is this elevator ever going to get there?' she seethed.

'Of course I'm happy to tell you what SE means,' replied McCools.

Thumble Tumble was beginning to think that this super intelligent creature was maybe not quite in the zone!

'But, you probably want to know the correct meaning for the T and H, otherwise the whole thing makes no sense at all!' he continued, waving his hands in the air.

'Er, yes. That would be great,' said Thumble Tumble, now sure McCools was a little bit wacky.

Just as the words left her lips, the elevator doors opened and McCools hobbled out into a circular room. Thumble Tumble noticed for the first time that McCools had one leg that was shorter than the other two, and this made him wobble every third step.

The circular room had no windows or doors, just row after row of book racks all sticking out from the wall to the centre of the room. Although, there were now very few books on the racks. They were mainly scattered over the floor, three books deep!

'This is the library,' announced McCools. 'And this is the devastation caused by your pounding.' He gestured to the piles of books lying everywhere.

'I'm sorry?' questioned Thumble Tumble.

'And so you should be,' McCools said pompously.

Thumble Tumble drew him a dagger of a look. But McCools completely ignored her and started picking up books from the floor. 'Too thin, too thick, too blue,' he muttered to himself as he dismissed the books one by one, tossing them over his shoulder as he searched.

'What *are* we looking for?' growled Thumble Tumble.

'How many times? The Tome of Dark Discovery!' McCools sighed, rolling his eyes, then resumed tossing books over his shoulder.

'I know what it's called. I need to know what it looks like!' screamed Thumble Tumble.

'There's no need to shout. I'm not deaf. All you had to do is ask!' he said. Then he continued his frenzied search. 'Nope, nope, nope.' He suddenly stopped. 'I do apologise, I completely forgot to answer you. H is for HERE, T is for THERE, and SE is for SOMEWHERE ELSE! Oh, and The Tome of Dark Discovery, it's about five inches thick with a black cover made from dragon skin. Please don't mention the cover to Jock, I don't want to upset him. It is a book of dark magic after all, and the Night Witches used to hunt dragons.'

'They still do,' said Thumble Tumble sadly. 'Watch out!' She grabbed a huge spell book up off the floor and then threw it straight back down.

'What is it?' said McCools, jumping back.

'It's a massive spider. It was just about to bite you!'

'You're more talented that you look, Thumble Tumble,'

said McCools as he pushed the spell book to one side. Underneath was a thick black book with a giant spider sitting right on top of it. The spider was smiling up at them, revealing its six razor-sharp fangs.

'This *is* The Tome of Dark Discovery,' said McCools as he picked the book up off the floor. 'The spider on the cover is just an illusion put there to scare people away from the book!'

'It looks pretty real to me,' said Thumble Tumble. 'Are you sure it's a fake?'

Just then, McCools threw his arm up in the air, waving it frantically above his head gripping the book with his hand. 'Help, help… get it off,' he yelled.

Thumble Tumble could see the spider's fangs glistening against the dark cover. She ran towards McCools but tripped over a pile of books lying on the floor. She fell flat on her face right at McCools' feet.

When she looked up, McCools was bent over holding onto his sides. 'I couldn't resist,' he chortled.

'Hysterical,' said Thumble Tumble as she clambered to her feet.

McCools started flicking through the pages of the book.

'Here it is,' he said. 'The Cauldron of Undry. The cauldron has the power to wake the dead, and also to return them to where they came from. There is no spell powerful enough to destroy the Mantigh. But the cauldron can return them to their deathly graves.'

'Where is this cauldron? asked Thumble Tumble.

'According to The Tome of Dark Discovery, the Cauldron of Undry is back with the Buddhists on the Holy Isle!' McCools announced dramatically.

## Chapter 10

## The Watcher

Torgle was seething at having to stand guard outside the little white cottage. He had been lurking in the shadows opposite the cottage for over an hour and now had goose bumps protruding all over his brown, gooey body. He couldn't feel his feet because of the cold and he was absolutely starving. He hadn't had any breakfast or lunch. And not a single bug had passed for him to at least have a snack! Grumbling noises started rising up from his stomach. The grumbling was soon so loud it began echoing around his head, making him feel disorientated.

Torgle glanced across at the cottage and momentarily forgot his hunger. He couldn't believe his eyes. It looked as though the cottage door was evaporating!

He rubbed his eyes, convinced he was hallucinating. When he looked back, the door had vanished, and, to his utter delight, he could see a tiny figure fluttering in the doorway. The little figure had bright red spiky hair…

'Mm, Flower Nymph,' he thought. 'Looks like I'll be having something to eat, after all!'

He edged his way out of the shadows. As he stepped onto the road, he could hear Serena's last words reverberating in his head:

'You will observe everyone who enters or leaves the cottage. You must not be seen. And, under no circumstances will you eat anyone. Do you understand me? I want to be sure you are fully aware of your orders. Because if you get them wrong, the next person to be eaten will be you!'

He paused for a moment. A single bead of sweat ran down his cheek, off his chin and onto the road. It reminded him of how the sweat had poured down his face when Serena had first towered above him with her so-called 'proposition'. *He would have to do exactly what she said, or she would eat him!* Not so much a proposition. More like a threat!

'I'm not afraid of an overgrown reindeer,' he told himself. The hunger pangs were giving him the extra courage needed to disobey Serena's orders.

'Besides, she'll never know!' he smirked to himself as he continued creeping across the road, which was now in complete darkness.

As he approached the open doorway, his eyes widened. He wasn't imagining this. There was a lone Flower Nymph fluttering there, just waiting to be devoured. He crouched down, ready to pounce.

He was poised waiting for the right moment to attack, when a huge foot landed three inches to his left. It gave him such a fright, he fell backwards into the shadows – not quite the majestic pounce he had planned.

Another foot came thumping down towards him, this time landing right on his big toe, crushing it. Tears of pain welled up in Torgle's eyes. He clenched his lips together so as not to let out a scream.

'I couldn't find Bessie anywhere,' said the owner of the offending foot. 'Where are the others?'

'They've gone to Goatfell Mountain,' said Blade.

'Oh great, that's all we need,' sighed Isla. 'An arrogant haggis, a gung-ho little witch and a sea dragon thrown in for good measure! We need to find them. How are your wings?'

'They're getting there,' said Blade.

'Good, you'll need them later. For now, you stay here in case Bessie shows up. I'm going to Goatfell.'

With that, Isla shot up into the night sky on her broom. Blade fluttered back towards the cottage. Just as he turned around, Torgle whipped his long black tongue towards the open doorway. As his tongue uncoiled, he could see the door reappearing from inside the frame. He desperately tried to re-coil his tongue. But the door was too fast. It closed like a kaleidoscope, trapping the tip of his tongue inside. And now he couldn't stop his tongue from rolling back up. As it did, it dragged his slimy body across the road and smashed him, face first, into the closed door.

He tried to pull his tongue free, but it wouldn't budge. He lay on the ground and pushed his feet against the door, but this only stretched his tongue back out.

As the magic porthole continued to try to close properly, his tongue was being squeezed tighter and tighter. Torgle continued pushing and pulling with all his might. Then all of a sudden, he went flying backwards.

His tongue was throbbing and swelling inside his mouth. He rolled it out to see what damage had been caused. When he caught sight of the end of his tongue, he keeled over right in the middle of the road.

'Wake up, you fool,' Serena whispered, prodding his body with her front hoof. 'You're supposed to be keeping watch, not snoozing.'

Torgle didn't say a word. He was too afraid to open his mouth. He knew Serena would be furious if she found out that the tip of his tongue had somehow managed to make its way inside the cottage!

'Well, has anyone come or gone?' she growled.

Torgle shook his head sheepishly.

'What, not a single person?' Serena probed.

Torgle shook his head again.

'That's funny, I'm sure I saw Isla leaving on her broom just a few moments ago.' Serena backed up onto her hind legs with her front hooves galloping in the air dangerously close to Torgle's head. 'Now let's try that again... has anyone come or gone, Torgle?'

Torgle tried to reply, but his tongue was now so swollen it was practically impossible to speak.

'They wen oo goa fe,' he slurred.

'What was that?' said Serena, her hooves now grazing his body.

He spoke as slowly and clearly as he could. 'I ed they wen oo Goatfell.'

'What is the matter with you, Torgle?' Serena snapped, lowering her front hooves back onto the ground. 'You sound like the cat has your tongue... literally!'

'I bit it,' he mumbled.

'That's typical. You're here to report comings and goings, but you can't speak because you've bitten your own tongue. You really are as stupid as you look! Are you trying to say they went to Goatfell?' she quizzed.

Torgle nodded.

'There's only one reason they would go to Goatfell Mountain.' Serena mused aloud. 'They must be going to see McCools. But what on earth do they want with that clever little Haggis? Torgle, you stay here,' she went on, 'and this time *do not* doze off on the job – or you just might not wake up again!'

Serena winked, but Torgle didn't miss the nasty glint in her eye.

As she trotted off into the darkness, Torgle said under his breath, 'Go on then... off to Mogdred, like a good little soldier.'

Torgle was cold, tired and very hungry. He had a crushed toe, a severely painful tongue and was most definitely no longer interested in Serena's 'proposition'.

He started hobbling along in the direction of Brodick Castle.

'Time to go home,' he sighed to himself as he limped along the road, 'back to my nice quiet pond.'

## Chapter 11

## *The Sleeping Gardener*

'Come out, come out, wherever you are,' Silusa sang as she glided through the corridors of the North Tower.

Buttercup could hear her distant chants as she lay, motionless, under the table in the living room of the dolls' house.

She was trying to remember the stories she had been told as a child, to see if there was anything in them that could help her! One particularly scary story popped into her head. It was 'The Tale of the Sleeping Gardener', the story told of a caretaker and a gardener who had once looked after Brodick Castle.

Murdo the gardener had grey hair and wrinkles that revealed his age. The smile lines around his mouth showed he had led a happy life, although there was also sadness in his eyes, from the loss of his beautiful wife.

Murdo and his wife had not been blessed with children, and so when she passed away, he offered to keep up the castle gardens if, in exchange, the local children could play in them.

It was a warm summer evening and Murdo was preparing the gardens for an amazing treasure hunt that was to take place the next day. He had hidden golden chocolate coins in amongst the tulips and candy jewels inside the rosebuds. The lawns were mowed and the flowerbeds looked like a giant rainbow bursting up from the ground.

Everything was ready. He packed up his tools and headed home, out through the castle gates. Just as he was about to lock the gates behind him, he realised he had forgotten to leave out the clues. They were still lying on a chest inside the castle!

'The children will be so disappointed,' he thought. He dropped his tool bag and ran back up to the castle. When he got there the doors were closed. He banged on the huge doors with his fists, but they didn't budge.

He stared at the locked doors and recalled the 'rules' that the housekeeper had set when he had first started working at the castle.

'Rule one, the North Tower is out of bounds – always!'

'Rule two, you must *never* enter the castle after the sun has set.'

'Rule three, do not attempt to break rules one or two.'

She had never given him an explanation as to why entry to the castle was forbidden after dark. But the look of fear in her eyes had sent such a chill down his spine that he knew he'd never break the rules!

That strange encounter was the first and last time

he had seen the housekeeper in the whole three years he had worked at the castle.

The sun had almost disappeared on the horizon. 'Probably just as well they're locked,' he thought to himself, remembering rule number two. Deep in contemplation, Murdo walked back along the dimly lit path towards the castle gates, wondering exactly who it was who locked the castle doors. He could smell the scent of daffodils wafting on the gentle breeze. He paused, convinced he could hear the sound of a girl's voice.

'*Come out, come out, wherever you are*,' she sang sweetly.

Murdo followed the sound, skirting around the castle walls, but there were no windows or doors for it to be coming from.

He ran his hands across the walls, feeling for any hidden passages, but there was nothing.

'*I'm waiting*,' the child sang out and giggled.

Murdo looked up and this time he could see a tiny window directly above him. He couldn't resist. He headed to the garden shed and returned a few moments later with a set of ladders. He placed the ladder against the wall and started to climb up. It was breaking the 'rules', but he had to see if there was a child inside the castle.

When he got to the open window, Murdo peered in to see the most delightfully decorated child's bedroom. Everything in tones of yellow, from the tulip curtains to the lettering on the big wooden toy box in the corner.

Murdo started to squeeze through the tiny window,

but as he hoisted himself through, the ladder went hurtling to the ground.

The force of Murdo's landing rolled him straight under the bed.

At that moment, the sweet voice of the child was replaced by a horrific cackle.

'We know you're in here!'

Murdo peeked from under the bed and there, circling above it, were two frightening creatures which looked like the ghosts of Night Witches. He knew instantly that he was in the company of Mantigh.

'We know you're here… Murdo!'

The cackling continued as the lid of the toy chest was thrown open and the two Mantigh floated in. As soon as they disappeared, Murdo put his hand up and grabbed the corner of the quilt. He pulled it under the bed and wrapped it around himself, then lay completely still.

The two Mantigh burst out of the toy chest. The first flew straight behind the curtains and started to rummage around. The second flew under the bed. She hovered just above the quilt that was encapsulating Murdo's body.

'Well?' screeched the first Mantigh.

'Not here,' the second squealed back.

'I know he's in the castle somewhere. Come on,' said the first Mantigh, and the pair turned to dust and floated out through the keyhole.

Murdo unwrapped himself from the quilt. He had guessed the Mantigh wouldn't see him because he knew they had poor eyesight, but he couldn't understand why they didn't feel his life force. Then he looked down. He was covered in grass, dirt and leaves from working in the garden all day.

'The debris from the garden must have masked my life force somehow,' he thought. 'But its protection won't last long. I need to find a way out of here!'

He crawled out from under the bed and headed over to the window. It was locked and the key was gone!

'So that's what she was doing behind the curtains!' Murdo said to himself.

He slowly walked over to the door and listened before turning the handle. It turned with ease. There was no sign of the Mantigh in the corridor.

Murdo knew his only options were to get out of the castle or stay hidden until morning. He tried every door and window he passed. They were all locked. With the Mantigh on his trail, he was sure they would catch up with him eventually.

'Time for Plan B… hide!' thought Murdo. He took off his boots and walked quickly along the corridor in his socks. There was a bunker inside the castle where they kept the coal. If the Mantigh couldn't feel his life force through grass, they definitely wouldn't feel it if he was surrounded by coal!

The coal bunker was dark and cold, but at least he was safe. Murdo waited silently in the dark. Hours passed and eventually he drifted off to sleep.

'Help me!'

The faint sound of a child whispering woke Murdo from his slumber.

He was trying to decide if he was still dreaming, or if he was awake and the whole experience had been a nightmare, when he heard the voice again.

'Help me!'

The sound was a little louder, but still a whisper. Murdo couldn't see anything in the pitch dark of the coal bunker.

'Please help me. I'm scared.' The child's voice was quivering.

'How did you get in here?' asked Murdo suspiciously, wondering if this was a Mantigh trap!

'I sneaked up to the North Tower. I know it was naughty, but I wanted to see if the stories of the dolls' house were true,' sobbed the child. 'I hid in here so I could go back and play with it, then I saw the scary ghosts.'

'Don't worry, I'm here now.' Murdo stretched his hand out in the dark. 'I'll get you out of here. But we need to be quiet. Shh.' He could feel his fingertips tingling. 'Is that you?' he whispered.

'Yes, it is.' Silusa's wails turned to laughter.

In the morning the children arrived for the treasure hunt, but there were no clues to lead them to the treasure. When they entered the castle, all they found was a trail of soot leading from the coal bunker to the North Tower.

They found Murdo lying at the foot of the stairs leading to the North Tower, covered head to toe in soot. At first, they thought he was asleep. But when they tried to wake him, they realised that he wasn't covered in soot, he had actually been turned to soot. Every morsel of life had been sucked from him.

His statue-like body was moved to the middle of the daffodil flower bed, where he still lies.

Buttercup snapped out of her daydream at the thought of poor Murdo's fate. She decided that staying in the Yellow Room was probably the safest option for now, and laid herself down. As her head touched the dolls' house floor, she could feel a tingling sensation on her cheeks.

## Chapter 12

## *Book Shower*

Isla landed gently on the cliff edge and dismounted from her broom. It had been snowing as usual and the ground was covered in crisp, fresh snow. The white carpet of snow was untouched, apart from a single set of hoof prints leading all the way up to a bright red door, which stood wide open.

Isla approached the doorway slowly. As she got closer, she could see patches of black smoke around the door frame. She had seen marks like this before, when her sister Lizzie had been killed. This was the stain left behind from a Night Witch's bolt.

She took her wand out of her pocket and raised it above her head, then stepped through the doorway into a wreckage of broken glass and porcelain scattered all over the floor. The remnants of a silver magic blanket lay ripped up in the corner.

Wand in hand, Isla cautiously walked along the hallway, pushing open every door as she passed, ready to strike. The sound of broken glass and porcelain crunching under her feet pierced through the silence. Isla waved her wand gently. 'ALEVIATUM!' she whispered, floating off the ground by a few centimetres and continuing along the hallway until she reached the elevator. She ascended to the first floor.

When the elevator doors opened, she was greeted by a sea of books strewn all over the floor. From the state of the place, Isla thought there must have been quite a struggle. Although, it struck her as strange that there was no sign of Night Witch bolts *inside* the house.

As Isla waded through the books, she noticed that some had been opened before being discarded.

'What were they looking for?' she wondered. 'What did Serena and the Night Witches want with McCool's books?'

Isla inspected every book rack from top to bottom, but found no clues as to what had happened, or what they had been looking for. She searched the rest of the house, room by room. Whoever the attackers were, they were long gone, along with Thumble Tumble, Jock and McCools!

Isla headed back outside, mounted her broom and set course for the cottage.

Serena fell off Gretch's broom and landed in a heap on a cold stone floor.

The room was in complete darkness.

'Did you find her?'

Serena recognised Mogdred's screech and the foul stench that always surrounded her.

There was a flash of light, then a candle ignited in the far corner of the room. Serena could just make out Mogdred's hunched figure in the flickering candlelight.

Mogdred had the same facial features as her daughters, long nose and straw hair, but she was much thinner. So thin, her body looked like a skeleton wrapped in a cloak.

She looked scrawnier and more hunched than Serena remembered from their last encounter.

'Did you hear me?' Mogdred barked and began to float across the stone floor towards Serena.

'It's unfortunate she doesn't *sound* any weaker!' thought Serena.

As Mogdred drew closer, Serena could see that her once white eyes were covered in blue veins and had huge rings of black skin around them, no doubt because she no longer had eyelids to protect them from the light. Even the dim candlelight seemed to be causing her excruciating pain.

'The house was deserted when we arrived,' reported Serena. 'Someone had attacked before us. The whole place looked like a battlefield. And for some reason, the library had been searched!'

'Who were these attackers?' snapped Mogdred.

'I don't know,' said Serena, 'but they were obviously looking for a book.'

'A book? What book?' howled Mogdred, now only centimetres away. Her foul exhalation almost over-whelmed Serena.

'I don't know what they were looking for. But, whatever it was, they found it!' said Serena, desperately trying to hold her breath.

'What makes you so sure?' asked Mogdred, running a long, black fingernail across Serena's cheek.

'There were still books on some of the book racks. If they hadn't found what they were looking for, all of the

*Mogdred*

books would have been on the floor,' gasped Serena.

'Very good,' sneered Mogdred, patting Serena on the cheek with her bony hand. 'Has the toad anything more to report?' she continued with another frightening sneer.

'He was nowhere to be found when I returned to the cottage,' replied Serena. 'I warned him what would happen if he left his post again.'

'That*sssss* good,' hissed Mogdred, running her black tongue around her lips. 'I might have felt guilty eating him, if he had not disobeyed me!' she cackled. 'Double the patrol around the cottage and find me that girl,' she yelled as she floated back towards the far side of the room.

Serena felt the apparating spell shoot through her body again, sending her hurtling through time and space.

When she came round, she was lying in the bushes

opposite the little white cottage. She stood up, smashed her hooves down on the ground and screamed in the air, 'N*oooo*!'

'Dear oh dear, will Serena *never* learn that I am not going to reveal the whereabouts of my lair to her?' Mogdred whispered to the young Deer Folk who was cowering in the corner, sobbing into her long violet hair.

Mogdred waved her hand over the large oval mirror hanging on the wall and the image of Serena faded into blackness.

## Chapter 13

## *Attack of the Thistle Pixies*

'What kept you?' McCools shouted up to Jock as he landed.

'I wasn't in a magic elevator, remember? I had to fly here!' snarled Jock.

'Well, you'd better take cover,' McCools shouted, just as a barrage of tiny spears came hurtling towards them.

'What's going on?' asked Jock.

'I think we've just come under attack,' said McCools. 'And, I'm pretty sure it's your fault!'

'What have I done?' said Jock, looking rather shocked.

'You arrived!' yelled McCools.

A second volley of spears came flying through the air towards them.

'What are these creatures?' gasped Thumble Tumble as she crawled through the long grass towards Jock, and the cover of his wings.

'Thistle Pixies,' replied McCools. 'Vicious little critters that protect the Buddhists.'

McCools and Thumble Tumble had landed on the

beach of the Holy Isle and headed inland through the thick grass. As soon as they touched the grass, their vibrations had sent a signal to the Thistle Pixies, alerting them to their presence.

The tiny pixies crept silently through the grass, forming a circle around the pair, their spears raised, ready to attack if they felt threatened. Although small, the spears were very effective. Made from thistles whittled down to a pinpoint at the tip, they were covered in razor-sharp thorns.

Jock's earth-shattering landing had been enough to send the pixies into attack mode. They had been thrown to the ground by the massive thud of Jock's feet touching down, which they took to be the first blow.

The spears were ripping into the thick skin on Jock's wings.

'We need to get out of here,' he hollered. 'My wings won't hold out much longer!'

'Get onto my broom,' Thumble Tumble shouted to McCools. McCools clambered onto the back of her broom and grabbed her around her waist.

'Ready?' shouted Jock. He lifted his wings to take off. But as soon as he left the ground, dozens more spears came hurtling through the air. He pushed his wings back down fast.

'Without the cover of my wings, you two will be torn to shreds,' he shouted down.

The tiny Thistle Pixies had long purple hair that stood straight up in the air, doubling their height to half a metre. Their bodies were covered in grass-stain and they wore little green tartan kilts. This allowed them to blend into the long grass, disguised as thistles.

*Kyle*

Kyle, the Chief of the Thistle Pixies, was now only a few centimetres away from them. He was roguishly handsome, with deep blue eyes and big pink lips. His kilt was different from the others. It was purple and black to represent the Thistle Clan.

'OK, what do we do now, genius?' Thumble Tumble asked McCools.

'Perhaps put up our hands?' he replied.

'What good will that do?' asked Thumble Tumble.

'Well, they might not kill us.' McCools nodded towards the ten Thistle Pixies now surrounding them, their spears aimed directly at their heads.

'Remove your wing,' Kyle called up to Jock.

Jock reluctantly lifted his wing and tucked it back into the side of his body.

'What are you doing on the Holy Isle?' Kyle demanded, prodding Thumble Tumble's arm with his spear.

'Ouch! We're here to see the Buddhists,' snapped Thumble Tumble.

'And what business do *you* have with the Buddhists?' quizzed Kyle.

McCools shook his head, indicating to Thumble Tumble *not* to say anything, but she replied defiantly, 'We're here to find the Cauldron of Undry!'

As soon as the words left her lips, Kyle opened his mouth and began to scream. Thumble Tumble fell to her knees, tears streaming down her face, she covered her ears with her hands. Jock and McCools were completely unfazed, but the high-pitched screech was impossible for Thumble Tumble to bear. She thought her eardrums were going to burst as the agonising pressure built up inside her head. She tried to cry out, but her voice had disappeared.

She collapsed, still clutching her ears, and just before she lost consciousness she glimpsed McCools taking something out of his scarf. It looked like a pepper shaker!

When she came round, Thumble Tumble felt as though she'd been whacked with a hockey ball. She tried to stand

106

up, only to fall back onto her knees.

'What happened?' she mumbled.

Eventually, she got onto her feet and commenced walking in a mini-circle with her hands out in front of her to help her balance. Through the mugginess, she was sure she could hear sneezing.

'A few seconds more, and your head would have exploded,' McCools said, 'so I had to resort to pepper!'

Thumble Tumble felt delirious.

'The Thistle Pixie screech is strong enough to make a witch's head explode,' McCools added.

Kyle was sneezing uncontrollably, jumping up and down and shaking his spear at McCools. His face had turned dark purple to match his hair and he was growling like a wild animal.

'There's no point in jumping up and down. I had *no* choice,' snapped McCools, waving his index finger at Kyle.

'I wouldn't have hurt her,' choked Kyle.

'I'm sorry, but I couldn't take that chance. Her head was about to blow off!'

'No it wasn't,' the little pixie retorted angrily. 'It was just a warning. Not powerful enough to burst anything. Just enough to give a bit of a headache!'

'Well, it certainly felt as though something was bursting!' Thumble Tumble interjected.

'OK, maybe a small head could have exploded,' conceded Kyle with a cheeky smile. He then blinked his eyes and he was gone, along with all of the other Thistle Pixies.

'Are you OK?' asked Jock.

'Yes, I'm fine,' replied Thumble Tumble. 'I just feel like I've scoffed ten scoops of ice cream! I've got the biggest brain freeze ever!'

During the commotion, they hadn't noticed how dark it had become. A beam of light passed over their heads and swung off to the far side of the island. It was the lighthouse on the peninsula of the Island sending out a warning beam for sailors travelling in the night.

'Oh no! We need to find that cauldron… and soon! If we don't get back to Brodick Castle before sunrise, Buttercup's fate will be on our hands,' said Thumble Tumble and she started making her way through the long grass towards the centre of the island.

The blades of grass barely parted as her slim form slid through them. Similarly, McCools' furry orange body glided between the blades. Jock, however, was like a two-metre wide lawn mower, ploughing through the grass, flattening it as he followed Thumble Tumble and McCools.

From the skies above, his mowing provided the perfect map of their route across the Holy Isle.

Despite this, the two Night Witches patrolling the sky above the Holy Isle still managed to miss them!

'Oh look,' sniggered Lumpsila dangling off of the edge of her broom. 'The Thistle Pixies are making a little pattern in the grass!'

'How sweet,' cackled her brother, Gorgour.

Gorgour and Lumpsila were Witch Trolls – half witch, half troll. Their mother was a particularly nasty Night Witch and their father was a Tree Troll. Unfortunately for them, it was their father's intelligence they had inherited. Tree Trolls are well known for their oversized heads and undersized brains!

As for their looks, Night Witches and Tree Trolls are

equally ugly and the siblings had a fair share of both parents' physical attributes.

They had crooked noses and murky grey skin from their mother and long thin bodies with giant heads, like a bulb on a stick, from their father.

'Let's have some fun,' said Lumpsila. And the two witches flew down from the cover of the clouds.

'Oh no, not again!' hollered Thumble Tumble as something whizzed past her head.

'Where are the little monsters this time? Can anyone see them?' she called back to Jock and McCools. Before either could reply, another object went hurtling past them, followed by three more.

All of the flying objects went straight over their heads and landed on the flattened grass behind Jock.

'That's not spears,' whispered McCools and he waved his hand, signalling to Thumble Tumble and Jock to keep low. 'They are Night Witch bolts. And I don't think they're aiming at us!'

'Oops!' cackled Lumpsila, as she fired bolt after bolt into the pattern she thought had been created by the Thistle Pixies.

'Not such a pretty pattern now,' Gorgour smirked.

The pair flew down into the path created by Jock's 'mowing', each of them running their wands along the sides, firing out sparks and setting the grass on fire.

'This is *vile*,' Lumpsila squealed with joy as she flew alongside Gorgour.

'I know. *So* vile. Why didn't we think of this yonks ago?' he replied.

The pair had in fact tried to set fire to the Holy Isle many times before. But the entire island is covered in a magical force-field that protects it from dark intruders. When they had attacked the island previously, their bolts had bounced off the force-field, setting themselves on fire!

The only reason their bolts were getting through now was because Jock's thunderous landing had caused a hairline crack in the force-field. The powerful combination of McCools' fur and Thumble Tumble's wand cutting through the grass had weakened the already vulnerable force-field, allowing the witches to fly along the path Jock had inadvertently created.

'Stay behind me,' shouted Jock. He stood up to his full height and spread out his enormous wings.

Lumpsila and Gorgour were having so much fun setting fire to the grass that they hadn't noticed Jock's massive body up ahead.

Jock closed his eyes and took a deep breath. As the air filled his lungs he could feel the water inside him being pushed up into his mouth, pressing his cheeks out like a hamster. He opened his eyes and took aim directly at Lumpsila and Gorgour.

'Stop!' shouted Thumble Tumble.

The two Witch Trolls halted in their tracks, only feet away from Jock's deathly water spray.

'The Thistle Pixies!' Thumble Tumble continued shouting. She pointed behind them to a group of Thistle Pixies who were standing in the path, trapped by flames on either side.

Jock spun around and released the jet hoses of water, extinguishing the fires on both sides of the pixies.

Lumpsila and Gorgour looked at one another in disbelief, then flew straight up into the night sky and disappeared into the clouds.

Jock generated another jet of water, but by the time he managed to spray it in the air, the Witch Trolls were long gone. All that was left behind was a huge black patch of smoking grass, right in the centre of the island.

'We may as well send out an invitation,' said McCools sarcastically. 'The Night Witches will be able to spot that smoke from miles away. As soon as those two morons report in, we're in trouble.'

'Don't get your knickers in a twist,' smiled Thumble Tumble. She took her wand out from her pocket. It was the size of a crayon until she waved it in the air, then it stretched out to its full length of thirty-three centimetres.

'EVAPORATUS INSTANTANEOUS!' she said, and swirled the wand above her head in a figure of eight.

A stream of twinkling green light left the tip of the wand and formed a small figure of eight right above her head.

The figure of eight floated over to the smoking patch of grass and started to grow. When it was the same size as the smoky patch below, it drifted down to the ground, and began to shrink again. As it shrunk, it gathered all of the smoke until it was just two green twinkles the size of two pennies. The two circles tilted on their sides and smacked together. As they collided, they sent out a huge wave of green smoke. The smoke wafted over the burnt grass, restoring it to its lushest green tones, then evaporated into thin air.

'I knew you were a clever little clogs,' smirked McCools.

'Wow, praise indeed, coming from you,' grinned Thumble Tumble.

'I wasn't talking to you,' said McCools. 'Good move,

Jock,' he continued, patting Jock's tail.

Thumble Tumble wanted to cast an evaporating spell on him. Gritting her teeth, she raised her wand. Her hand was shaking.

'Thank you,' said Kyle taking hold of the tip of her wand. He had appeared from nowhere and was now standing right in front of her. 'If you hadn't spotted my men trapped in the path, they would have been killed,' he went on, lowering her wand as he spoke. 'How can we ever repay you?'

'We really need to speak with the Buddhists,' Thumble Tumble said anxiously.

'Then so you shall,' said Kyle. He turned on his heels and began walking back towards the shoreline. 'Follow me.'

## Chapter 14

## *Groucho's Gauntlet*

They had been walking for ages in what seemed like a giant circle.

Thumble Tumble wanted to know where they were being taken. She walked up behind Kyle and put her hand out to tap him on the shoulder. Just then, he stopped so suddenly that she almost walked straight into his back.

'We're here,' he announced, and pointed his spear at a thick clump of grass a few feet ahead.

'Exactly where are we?' asked Thumble Tumble, frowning at the clump of grass.

'The entrance,' said Kyle. 'You want to meet the Buddhists, so you have to enter the temple.'

Thumble Tumble walked towards the clump of grass and placed her right toe on top of it. She then disappeared, right in front of their eyes.

'What have you done?' yelled Jock as he bore down on Kyle.

'She's gone to meet the Buddhists, just as you asked,' Kyle grinned cheekily.

'We saved you! Why would you trick us?'

'Don't worry, Jock. It's not a trick,' said McCools, gently pushing Jock's head back from Kyle's face. 'There's a secret tunnel that leads to the Buddhists Temple. But, only one person can travel through the tunnel each day. This is to protect the sanctuary of the temple from the Night Witches.'

Thumble Tumble felt as though she was falling through a huge flume, but instead of going down, she was going up! Her feet pointing out in front of her, she slid up to the left, then across horizontally before sliding up to the right.

The flume was pitch black inside and something that felt like tiny fingers stuck out of the sides of the flume, wiggling at her as she slid through it.

She soared rapidly on the upwards part of the slide, then slowed right down as she slid horizontally. The stop-start motion was playing havoc with her stomach. Up and across she travelled – so many times, she lost count.

Finally, she came hurtling out of the flume and landed at Brother Groucho's feet. As soon as she hit the floor she threw up.

'Oh no,' groaned Groucho. He pulled a large book out from the sleeve of his cloak.

Groucho was a tall thin man and the sour expression on his face matched his name. He was wearing a long grey cloak that came all the way down to his bare feet. There was a rope tied around his waist.

His globe-shaped eyes almost popping out of his head, he threw the book up in the air with one hand, ready to whack Thumble Tumble over the head.

Thumble Tumble was still coughing and spluttering on the floor. She raised her hand in the air to protect herself.

'Oh my goodness, I almost flattened you,' said Groucho lowering the book. He rubbed his eyes. The glare from the light bouncing off Thumble Tumble's ring had dazzled him.

He bent down to help her to her feet.

'I'm so sorry, I thought you were some sort of Dark Witch. I didn't realise you're green!'

'I'm not green,' spluttered Thumble Tumble. 'Well, not usually!' She looked down and realised she was covered in green vomit. 'It was the flume ride. It made me feel...' Just the thought of the scary slide made Thumble Tumble feel nauseous again.

'Take your time,' said Groucho, carefully stepping over the puddle of vomit.

Thumble Tumble sat on the floor for a few moments until the colour reappeared in her cheeks. She then took out her wand and waved it in the air. 'Spick and span as quick as you can' she chimed.

Nothing happened!

'I'm afraid your magic doesn't work inside the temple,' said Groucho. 'Here, use this.' He produced a small facecloth from the other sleeve of his cloak.

'That's convenient,' said Thumble Tumble. 'Do you always carry a facecloth in your cloak?'

'Yes, pretty much,' replied Groucho in a cheery tone. 'You never know when you might need one!'

Despite the permanent frown on his forehead and a mouth that turned down at the sides like a trout, Groucho was really pleasant and not grouchy in the slightest.

When Thumble Tumble had wiped the last traces of vomit from her dress, she realised that Groucho had stopped mid-swing, when about to plonk her with his book.

'Why did you stop?' she asked. 'You know, from plonking me with your book!'

'Your ring,' he blurted out. 'The light reflecting off it blinded me at first, but then I recognised it. You're a little younger than I was expecting, although I don't know why I thought you'd be older. It is only eight years since the battle.'

'Battle, what battle?' queried Thumble Tumble.

'Oh, we don't have the time to get into that just now. I understand you're here for the Cauldron of Undry,' said Groucho, quickly changing the subject.

'How do you know that?'

'It's what everyone comes here for,' he said, smiling, and beckoned her to follow him along a huge corridor.

For the first time, Thumble Tumble noticed how beautiful her surroundings were.

The floors and walls were covered in marble. The corridor was lined with golden pillars stretching up ten metres to a ceiling decorated with breathtaking frescos depicting battles against the Night Witches. There was even a fresco illustrating the battle at Lochranza Castle, where she and Jock had helped the Deer Folk defeat Mogdred.

As they continued, Thumble Tumble realised there were no doors or windows inside the temple. It was just one long corridor.

'Is it far?' she asked Groucho.

'Not far now,' he replied, and continued walking with his head down. He seemed to be muttering to the marble floor.

Thumble Tumble looked back up at the ceiling. Now the frescos were no longer of battle scenes. Instead, literally hundreds of portraits of Buddhists were staring down at them. Some with hair, some completely bald. Some had blue eyes, some green, others brown. There were moustaches, beards, hats and bows.

No two portraits were the same, but they all had one thing in common. In every picture, the figure was holding a black cauldron.

'This is where I leave you,' said Groucho, stopping.

Thumble Tumble looked around her, but there was no door or window for her to go through.

'What do I do next?' she enquired, still looking around at the seemingly empty corridor.

'You'll see,' said Groucho and he turned and walked back the way they had come.

Thumble Tumble glanced ahead then turned back for guidance. But Groucho was now miles off in the distance. Desperately trying to work out what she was supposed to do, she wondered if there was some hidden message in the portraits. Maybe a secret symbol, or the magical words to a spell?

As she stared up at the ceiling, she heard a muffled sound, like water slowly dripping onto the floor. The noise began to get louder, but still she couldn't make out what it was.

She lay down on the floor to get a closer look at whatever was falling.

'*Arrghh*!' she screamed and jumped straight back up onto her feet.

The thin blue veins weaving their way through the floor were not actually part of the marble at all. They were lines of tiny blue ants. As Thumble Tumble stared down at them, the legion of tiny ants marched to either side of the corridor and formed two straight lines. When their manoeuvre was complete, silence reigned again. It was so still, Thumble Tumble could hear herself breathing.

The calm was suddenly broken by an almighty explosion. The blast sent Thumble Tumble crashing to the ground. Fragments of dust and debris went flying everywhere, making it impossible to see what had caused the explosion.

Thumble Tumble was picking herself up when a second blast detonated. This time she was smashed against the wall and slid sideways down to the ground and landed on a giant black cauldron.

She looked up to the nightmarish sight of the Buddhists in the portraits throwing their cauldrons down at her. She pointed her wand towards the ceiling and tried shouting 'STILLAMOMENTUM!'

Boom! Another cauldron came crashing down right beside her, covering her in a spray of rubble. 'Oh no, magic doesn't work in here,' she remembered.

Thumble Tumble dived to one side as another cauldron landed exactly where she had been standing. She leapt to her feet and started sprinting along the corridor, a cascade of cauldrons crashing behind her.

A huge cauldron came rolling along the corridor like a ball down a bowling alley. Just in time, Thumble Tumble slapped herself against the wall and sucked her tummy in as it went past, skimming the hem of her dress.

'Phew,' she gasped out loud, and sank down in relief. 'Oh no!' she hollered, and dived back up. 'Are you OK?' she called down to the legions of ants. 'Did I crush anyone?'

The ants hadn't budged. Not a single one was out of

place. They were all still standing in a perfectly straight line along the edge of the floor.

Just then, another cauldron came at her, bouncing from wall to wall like a giant pinball.

Thumble Tumble bent down. 'Get onto my hat,' she shouted to the ants.

But the ants didn't respond.

'Hurry up, please get on?' she pleaded.

The little blue line held fast without a flinch.

Thumble Tumble just had time to leap out of the way of the pinball cauldron before it crashed into the wall, sending chunks of marble crashing onto the floor.

Thumble Tumble darted back and threw her hands out above the ants, hoping to protect them from the falling marble. The ants remained in perfect formation while she waved her hands frantically, batting away the falling pieces of marble from landing on them.

The Buddhist right above her head now dropped his giant cauldron. It fell silently through the air. The force of its impact made the floor quake. Thumble Tumble fell and as the back of her head hit the floor she looked up to see a sheet of blue ants floating above her. Hundreds of them had linked together, forming a shield that completely covered her body. Cauldron after cauldron came hurtling down, reverberating against the blue bubble surrounding her.

After a while, Thumble Tumble clambered to her feet. She tentatively walked along the corridor. The ant shield moved with her as though it was an extension of her own body as she slowly made her way down the corridor.

When she reached the entrance, the ants marched down from the shield, looking like a big ball of wool unwinding.

Within minutes, the shield had transformed back into a thin blue line stretching back along the corridor towards the portraits.

Thumble Tumble could hear clapping coming from inside the wall beside her – and then Groucho emerged out of the wall, clapping his hands.

'Well done, well done. I knew you could make it,' he said, tapping Thumble Tumble gently on the shoulder. 'Only those purest of heart return from the gauntlet, and I knew you were the moment I saw you. Well, I was ninety nine percent sure,' he smiled. 'Come on, let's get you that cauldron!'

'Is that it?' asked a startled Thumble Tumble.

'Unless you'd rather go back in to run the gauntlet again… this time without the help of my ants,' he said looking down at her with raised eyebrows.

'No thanks,' she said quickly, shaking her head.

'Very well then,' said Groucho, and placed the palm of his left hand on the spot he'd just emerged from.

'What's the magic word?' a sharp little voice came from behind the wall.

'Oh, come on Hibert, let us through,' sighed Groucho.

'I'm afraid I can't let you through without the magic word,' insisted the person behind the wall.

'Hibert, let us through right now,' demanded Groucho.

'Nope. I'm sorry, but you know the rules. You made them,' Hibert snapped back.

'Fine,' Groucho conceded.

'MAGNIFISO, HIBERTSO, LETUSINO!'

He turned to Thumble Tumble and whispered, 'Hibert is a little fastidious!'

A tiny blue spark appeared where Groucho's palm had

been. The spark burst into flame, evaporating the wall as it flared. An opening then appeared as the flame subsided.

The room behind the wall was nothing like the grand corridor they were standing in. It was a small box-room with wooden floors and grey walls.

'Come on then, we've not got all day. I mean, night,' said Hibert.

Hibert was half the height of Groucho and twice the width. He was completely bald, except for the three single strands of brown hair that were smoothed over his head. He had thick bushy eyebrows that stuck out at the sides of his round face. And like Groucho he was dressed in a grey robe with a rope tied around the middle. Only, Hibert's rope was so tight it made him look like a human egg-timer!

Thumble Tumble noticed a pentagon drawn on the floor in the centre of the room, with symbols and strange words written around the sides.

'It's old magic,' explained Groucho. 'It's from the time of the great coven, before Mogdred and her army of Night Witches unleashed their evil upon the world.'

Thumble Tumble stared at him blankly for a few seconds before finding her voice.

'Groucho, can you tell me about the coven? I think it had something to do with my mother's death. But no one will speak to me about how, or why, she died.' A single tear rolled down Thumble Tumble's cheek as she spoke.

Groucho shook his head apologetically.

'The coven existed to preserve the balance of good and evil,' piped up Hibert. 'Balance is needed, as without good there can be no evil, and vice versa. This has always been the way. But one witch was so blinded by her greed for power that she put the whole world in jeopardy. Her name was Mogdred. So great was the fear of Mogdred's ambition, that the Witch Council created a "Protector". One witch was chosen, and upon her was bestowed the powers of all witches. Her quest was to destroy Mogdred. Your mother was that Protector.'

'But how did she die if she was so powerful?' sobbed Thumble Tumble, tears flowing down her cheeks. She looked longingly at Hibert for an answer.

'We don't know,' sighed Hibert. 'Maybe it was just her time, or she was trying to protect someone else.'

'Who?' cried Thumble Tumble. 'Who was she protecting?'

'That's enough, Hibert,' Groucho intervened. 'We don't know what happened, Thumble Tumble,' he continued. 'All we know is that your mother maimed Mogdred, which is why she disappeared.'

'Is that why she ordered the death of all Sea Dragons?' asked Thumble Tumble, her voice trembling.

'Your mother was an amazing witch,' said Groucho. 'She would not hesitate to lay down her life to save another. She died trying to put an end to Mogdred's tyranny. If she hadn't maimed Mogdred, your friend Jock probably wouldn't be alive today! Now, dry those eyes and please step into the pentagon.'

When Thumble Tumble stepped into the pentagon, Groucho reached into the sleeve of his robe and brought out a tiny cauldron, only two centimetres in diameter.

'Here,' he said, and placed the miniature cauldron in Thumble Tumble's hand. 'Please try to bring it back to us in one piece.'

Thumble Tumble felt the ground beneath her feet

disappear and she began to slip through the air.

'How does it work?' she called out.

'The cauldron will lead you,' Groucho shouted back.

The pentagon had disappeared completely, dropping her feet-first back into the dark tunnel. This time she was sliding downwards. Down and across she zigzagged, at what felt like a hundred kilometres an hour, heading for an exit that looked the size of a pinhole!

As she hurtled towards the dot of light, it started to get bigger.

Thumble Tumble came shooting out of the entrance to the tunnel like an arrow from a bow and flew high up into the sky, feet-first, before her momentum ran out and she came crashing back to earth head-first.

'*Arrghh*!' she screamed as she plummeted towards the ground.

She bounced back up in the air three times before tumbling off Jock's outstretched wing.

'Thanks for the trampoline, Jock,' she gasped. 'That could have been pretty nasty for my head!'

'No problem,' said Jock. 'Did you find the cauldron?'

'I did' she said hesitantly. 'But…'

'But what?' probed McCools.

'I'm not sure what to do with it!' she replied.

'Don't worry about that now. Let's just get the cauldron to Brodick Castle before it's too late.'

## Chapter 15

## *Hidden in the Clouds*

Torgle hung in mid-air, the chains around his wrists hoisting his arms up above his head.

Mogdred pointed her long black finger and shot another lightning bolt straight into his stomach. At the excruciating pain, Torgle's huge eyes opened and he tried to say something, but his lips seemed to be stuck together. Some sort of invisible muzzle on his face was holding his mouth shut but he could still smell the stench rising from the dungeon floor below.

'Your mouth will open when you're ready to tell me *ssss*omething,' hissed Mogdred.

Torgle had been limping back towards the pond, mumbling to himself, when Sloth and Gretch had spotted him on a routine fly-by over Brodick Castle.

'My, my, what do we have here?' sniggered Sloth, as she flew down to confront the exhausted toad.

Torgle was so tired and sore, he could barely lift his head to look at her, let alone run.

The last thing he remembered was Sloth hitting him with an 'apparating' bolt, not a particularly strong one, but he was so weak it knocked him out.

'Well, have you got any information for me?' Mogdred drew closer to Torgle tapping her long, black fingernails together in front of her face.

Her breath was vile. Gasping for air, Torgle summoned his last morsel of energy to lift his head.

Mogdred flicked her right hand and the invisible muzzle was gone. Torgle gulped down a huge gasp of air. He could feel his heart racing as the oxygen filled his lungs.

'They're looking for something,' he panted.

'And?' barked Mogdred.

'It… It's on the Holy Isle.' Mogdred moved so close to Torgle he could feel her cold breath on his cheek. She leaned in and whispered in his ear, 'Now, can you tell me something I don't know?'

She ran a ragged fingernail down his cheek and suddenly stabbed it into his double chin, tilting his head back.

Torgle closed his eyes, waiting for the fatal death bolt.

A sharp pain shot through his head. Then, he heard screaming!

This was not what he had expected to feel like at all. He thought he'd feel numb. Instead, he was still aching from head to toe. Torgle opened his eyes to the most bizarre scene.

Gorgour and Lumpsila had come into the dungeon, both travelling so fast they couldn't stop. Gorgour managed to pull his broom up, which sent him crashing into the ceiling. But Lumpsila's broom was too heavy for her. She grabbed at the handle with all her might, but lost her grip and was lobbed off, while the broom continued, riderless, until it slammed into Mogdred's back.

Mogdred was thrown forward, pushing Torgle back against the wall. The pain he felt shooting through his head was when it banged against the wall, not her death bolt.

Mogdred flew up in a rage and grabbed Lumpsila by the throat.

'Let her go,' demanded Gorgour.

Mogdred turned and fired a death bolt straight at him. He ducked just in time for the bolt to fly over his head. Mogdred began to tighten her grip around Lumpsila's scrawny neck and lifted her up off the floor.

'We have news about Thumble Tumble,' Gorgour said hastily.

Mogdred glared at him. She was still choking Lumpsila, whose feet were now dangling in the air a few centimetres off the ground.

'She was on the Holy Isle. She was with the Sea Dragon and that meddling haggis, McCools. They were looking for the Cauldron of Undry.'

'How do you know that?' spat Mogdred.

'We were hiding,' smirked Gorgour. 'They thought we'd gone, but we waited in the clouds, right above their heads. We heard, everything!'

'Do they have the cauldron?' asked Mogdred.

'Yes. And they're on their way to Brodick Castle with it right now.'

Mogdred released her grip around Lumpsila's throat and let the Witch Troll fall to the floor.

'That's interesting. If they don't know that we know about the cauldron, they won't be expecting us. And the cauldron will be mine at last!'

'You'll also get rid of Thumble Tumble and her pathetic friends,' cackled Lumpsila, feeling brave enough to speak.

Mogdred just glowered at her.

'Get my daughters. We'll meet in the castle grounds,' she barked, then snapped her fingers in the air and disappeared.

Gorgour and Lumpsila headed up the stairs from the dungeon to find Gretch and Sloth. The sisters were in the kitchen, tucking into a feast of stale bread, bugs and worms.

'What do *you* want?' spluttered Sloth.

A small green beetle escaped from her mouth as she spoke and managed to crawl all the way down her chin before being swiped back in with her long black tongue.

'We've to go to Brodick Castle. Mogdred's orders,' announced Lumpsila warily.

Sloth and Gretch were every bit as ruthless as their mother, and took great pleasure in bullying their peers. Lumpsila, who had been the focus of their bullying in the past, flinched every time one of them came near her, which amused the sisters no end.

Gorgour, on the other hand, was an even bigger bully than the two sisters.

'Oi, you heard her. Stop filling your ugly faces with worms and get your brooms,' he ordered.

The sisters waddled over to the wall to retrieve their brooms and the four witches flew out of the window into the night.

Torgle waited until he was sure the castle was empty. He then opened his mouth and rolled his tongue up his arm to his wrist. The tip of his severed tongue was smothered with gooey saliva that dribbled onto the chains gripping his wrist.

After a few seconds his hand started to slide through the chains, then it fell to his side. Torgle swung helplessly from side to side, dangling from the ceiling with the chains digging deeper and deeper into his trapped wrist, cutting off the circulation.

He took a deep breath and whipped his head across, throwing his tongue onto the chain and licking it frantically.

'Come on… please slide,' he pleaded inside his head.

His chubby hand gradually slipped through the chain and he landed on the floor with a thud.

## Chapter 16

## *Fairy Dew*

Thumble Tumble flew down through the clouds towards the cottage, closely followed by Jock. They landed in front of the door at the same time as Isla arrived from Goatfell.

'Thank goodness you're OK,' Isla said as she slipped gently off of her broom. 'I thought you'd been attacked by the Night Witches and that traitor, Serena! McCools' house is completely trashed, and I spotted hoof-prints in the snow.'

'Oh, the destruction of my house was actually your niece's work,' said McCools huffily, as he climbed down from Thumble Tumble's broom.

'Ah McCools, just as moody as ever,' smiled Isla. 'So good to see you,' she gushed, and threw her arms around his fluffy orange body.

McCools squirmed out of Isla's grip and continued with his rant: 'Although, I can't account for any hoofprints.'

'There were scorches of Night Witch bolts on the door too,' added Isla.

'Mm, they must have paid me a visit after we left for

the Holy Isle,' frowned McCools. 'Looking for this pair, no doubt.' He pointed towards Thumble Tumble and Jock.

'But how did the Night Witches know they had gone to see you?' asked Isla.

McCools was now pacing back and forth in front of the cottage, kicking at the road with his three feet, one at a time.

'Are you with us McCools?' said Isla.

McCools didn't reply. He just continued staring at his feet and stomping up and down the road.

'Oh come on, McCools. Snap out of it!' shouted Isla.

McCools didn't respond. Instead, he plonked himself down right in the middle of the road and gazed at the ground.

'This is no time for sitting around,' growled Thumble Tumble, through gritted teeth.

'Dribble!' said McCools.

'I beg your pardon?' Thumble Tumble snapped back.

'Dribble!' he repeated.

'Look, I've had just about all I can take of your obnoxious behaviour,' said Thumble Tumble.

McCools didn't even glance up at the angry little witch marching towards him. He just ran his index finger along the ground and then rubbed it on his tongue!

Thumble Tumble stopped in her tracks.

'What is this crazy haggis up to now?'

'It's toad dribble!' gagged McCools as he started spitting brown, slimy goo onto the ground. 'It's horrible,' he screeched, trying to wipe off the offending mucus.

'Take this – quick,' said Isla, pulling a small bottle the size of a stamp out of her pocket. The bottle contained a bright pink liquid. 'It's Fairy Dew.' She pulled out the cork and pushed the tiny bottle into McCools' hand.

He took a huge gulp, then gasped, 'Thank goodness,' before taking another swig.

'That was close,' said Isla sternly. 'You're lucky I had some Fairy Dew on me… oh, never mind. At least you're OK,' she continued, shaking her head in disapproval.

'I know. I just totally forgot how bad toad's slime can be,' said McCools as he knocked back the last dregs of the pink liquid from the bottle.

'So, it doesn't taste very nice,' said Thumble Tumble, mimicking McCools voice. 'I don't know what all the fuss is about!'

'Haven't you taught this child anything?' McCools snapped at Isla.

'Yes, we have,' she replied in an equally sharp tone.

'Well, you wouldn't know it!' McCools retorted.

'That's the whole idea… remember?' Isla's face was now scarlet and the vein on her forehead was pulsing.

'Yes, I do remember,' shouted McCools. 'But now that Mogdred knows who she is, perhaps it's time to stop hiding the truth from her, and start training her?'

'She's too young,' Isla yelled at the top of her lungs. 'We don't want to lose her too!' Isla was glaring at McCools, her eyes filled with rage.

'You need to *stop* arguing,' cried Blade, who had hobbled out to find out what all the commotion was. 'We've got the Night Witches to contend with… we don't need to fight one another as well!'

'I'm sorry,' said McCools, lowering his voice again. 'But I don't think Mogdred will be forgiving just because Thumble Tumble's only nine!'

'I know,' said Isla. 'I'm sorry too. I just can't bear the

thought of anything happening to her.'

All five of them stood in the doorway for a moment, before Blade broke the silence.

'I think I know who this dribble belongs to! It's got to be Torgle! The Flower Nymphs are all in a flap because he tried to eat Lily this morning. Unfortunately for him, all he got was a mouthful of pollen, so he's not happy!'

'If Torgle has been spying on us, it's safe to assume that Mogdred knows we were looking for the Cauldron of Undry!' said McCools. 'That explains why the Night Witches were at my house. They were looking for The Tome of Dark Discovery too!'

'Mogdred has been after that cauldron for a long time,' said Isla in a sombre voice, 'and she'll do anything to get it… look at what happened to Silusa!'

'What happened to Silusa?' asked Blade.

'The Mantigh are what happened!' replied McCools gravely. 'After she used the cauldron to create those deathly creatures, it vanished and she's been obsessed about finding it again ever since!'

'Poor Silusa,' said Thumble Tumble sadly.

'Silusa is no longer with us,' said McCools, speaking to Thumble Tumble in a soft voice for the first time since they had met. 'The Mantigh are pure evil. When we die, our soul splits into two parts. For a brief moment, the good and the bad in us separate. There was a tiny part of Silusa that was bad, and that, sadly, is the *only* part the cauldron brought back! The "real" Silusa died a long time ago,' Isla explained. 'Whatever happens, we *cannot* let Mogdred get her hands on the cauldron. With its power, she could destroy the whole world!'

Thumble Tumble slipped her hand into the long

pocket of her dress and pulled it back it out, with her fist closed. She opened her hand slowly to reveal a tiny black cauldron.

'Well we'd better take good care of this then,' she said.

'*You* have it!' gasped Isla.

'Let's just say I managed to persuade the Buddhists to let us *borrow* it,' said Thumble Tumble, grinning. She popped the tiny cauldron back into her pocket.

'We need to get that to the castle,' said Blade.

'That we do,' Isla agreed. 'But Mogdred will be waiting for us, with the full force of her army behind her.'

'I'm counting on it,' winked McCools, as he headed into the cottage.

Isla followed McCools inside and the pair of them rolled out a map of Brodick Castle on the kitchen table.

'I still don't know what all the fuss was about,' Thumble Tumble whispered to Jock, who was now sitting in front of the cottage, giving his huge wings a well-deserved rest.

'It's poisonous,' said Jock. 'Toad's dribble is so lethal it can kill you in a few moments without the antidote.'

'And, I take it, the antidote is Fairy Dew?' said Thumble Tumble, shrugging her shoulders in dismay.

'Yip,' nodded Jock.

'I really don't know anything, do I?' she mumbled as she went into the cottage to help the others plan Buttercup's escape.

## Chapter 17

## *Assault on Brodick*

Buttercup lay motionless on the floor under the coffee table, willing it to stay put.

Her lips were tightly pressed together and she was trying to breathe through her nose without her body moving. She knew that even the slightest change in the air could alert the Mantigh to her hiding place. That included the invisible ripples caused by breathing!

As she lay there, she noticed that the tingling sensation on her cheeks was getting stronger. At first it had felt like pins and needles, but now it was more like daggers piercing through her skin. The pain was agonising, but still she didn't move.

The room temperature was also dropping. It sank so low, that a little white cloud formed just above her face as her breath condensed in the freezing air.

To Buttercup, it looked like a big white arrow pointing down at her!

'Come out, come out, wherever you are!' Silusa's eerie tones echoed through the keyhole.

It was now pitch black outside. Even the stars couldn't penetrate the dark skies over Brodick Castle. This was because Mogdred's army of Night Witches had surrounded the castle from above.

Sloth and Gretch had led the patrol from the north, while Gorgour and Lumpsila had flown in from the south. Dozens of black-cloaked figures hovered silently in the night sky.

Serena had ordered the ground troops to dig a trench a few metres in front of the castle doors – the only way in or out of the building – and then ordered it to be covered. Now all they had to do was wait for Thumble Tumble to show up with the cauldron – although, she did think it was a bit strange that Mogdred hadn't yet appeared. She was sure Mogdred would want to be there in person when the cauldron was surrendered. Serena started to feel a little bit uncomfortable with the whole situation. She didn't trust Mogdred one bit, and wouldn't be surprised if she had set her up, as bait!

'I'm going to have a look around the castle grounds to make sure we haven't missed anything,' Serena said to the burly Night Witch who was her second in command. 'You stay here. And whatever you do, *do not* take your eyes off of those doors.'

Serena jumped up out of the trench, leaving the ground troops poised to attack.

As she crept slowly through the gardens towards the castle gates, Serena had the feeling she was being followed. She ducked out of sight into a bush and waited to find out the identity of her stalker. No one appeared.

She stood in silence for a further ten minutes before she decided it was her imagination playing tricks on her and continued heading for the castle gates, trotting as quietly as she could. She knew if Mogdred caught her leaving the battlefield, she'd be a goner for sure!

Just as that thought passed through her mind, she heard a twig snap behind her.

She whirled round, but she couldn't see anything in the blackness. A cold shiver ran through her body.

'Hello, Serena,' a voice whispered from the dark.

Serena froze to the spot.

'LUMINATI!' said Bessie, her wand pointing at Serena's forehead. 'What a surprise bumping into you here.'

'I can explain,' Serena said, looking around in a panic.

But, before she could utter another word, there was an earth-shattering explosion as death bolts started raining down on the castle grounds.

Jock swung his huge wings up like a shield. The death bolts were bouncing off them, into the trenches where the Night Witches were still lying in wait.

'Why aren't the bolts killing him?' screamed Gretch.

'Because they *knew* we were here,' roared Mogdred.

Mogdred could see Isla standing beside Jock with her wand aimed at the giant Sea Dragon's wings. She was clenching her wand with both hands as it shook uncontrollably from the powerful spell she was casting onto him.

'Get lower. Aim for his body,' Mogdred hollered to Gretch and Sloth.

'I don't know how much longer I can keep this up,' Jock panted, as he stood in front of the castle doors.

'Just a few more moments, that's all we need,' Isla said, straining to speak whilst still controlling her spell.

As instructed, Gretch and Sloth flew down and positioned themselves on either side of Jock's body. He blew out a massive jet of water, but it didn't get anywhere near them. They were too far round. He would need to lower his wings to turn his head around far enough to reach them. And that's exactly what they were waiting for!

Mogdred flew down from the clouds and hovered right above Isla. She knew Isla couldn't defend herself while she was still casting the force-field spell. She cackled with excitement at the thought of killing the undefended witch below her.

Her plan was perfect! She would take out Isla, destroying the force-field at the same time. This would then clear the way for Gretch and Sloth's death bolts to kill Jock.

She pointed her long black finger towards Isla's head and shouted out, '*Now!*'

All three Night Witches fired their death bolts.

As soon as Mogdred's bolt left her fingertip, Isla dropped her wand and the images of Isla and Jock vanished.

'N*oooo!*' screamed Mogdred.

Sloth's death bolt travelled straight through the air where Jock had been standing. The bolt landed on the ground and exploded in a cloud of ash.

A split second later, Gretch's death bolt hit, only this time it wasn't the ground. The death bolt seared through Sloth's left arm, chopping her hand clean off.

Sloth screamed in agony as she fell from her broom, clutching onto the smouldering stump with her other hand.

Mogdred fired an apparating bolt that hit Sloth, seconds

before she went crashing into the ground. She aimed another at Gretch, and then the three witches disappeared into the night.

## Chapter 18

## Bridge 'Club'

'Can I please put my wings down now?' pleaded Jock.

'Yes,' sighed Isla, who was now lying flat out on the grass beside the gates at the entrance of the castle grounds.

'I just hope we kept the hologram going long enough to give Thumble Tumble time to get inside,' she gasped.

Isla had cast the hologram spell as a distraction to allow Thumble Tumble and McCools to get into the castle without being spotted by the Night Witches.

The pair were positioned in the clouds above the North Tower, waiting for the Night Witches to open fire.

McCools had studied the plans for the castle and found a way in... Santa style, down the chimney!

As soon as the witches started firing, Thumble Tumble flew them down.

'Jump!' she shouted when they were directly over the chimney pot.

The pair let go of the broom and whizzed down the chimney shaft, banging off the sides as they fell.

Thumble Tumble came hurtling out first, landing in a

pile of soot. A second later, McCools landed head-first on her back. The pair rolled out of the fireplace, covered in soot from head to toe.

Thumble Tumble wiped the soot out of her eyes.

'Where to?' she asked anxiously.

'We need to get to Silusa's bedroom,' said McCools, struggling not to laugh at Thumble Tumble's hilarious 'panda face'!

Thumble Tumble threw him a dagger of a look.

'Hmm, this way,' he said, pointing over to a door and speaking in a tone that reflected the seriousness of their situation.

They had landed inside one of the castle's grand drawing rooms. A massive crystal chandelier hung from the ceiling. Plush leather chairs were dotted around the room and in the centre a card table had been set up for a game of Bridge.

They slowly walked towards the door, taking care not to touch anything.

'It seems OK in here!' Thumble Tumble said.

Suddenly, the cards that had been lying on the table flipped up onto their sides and waddled to the edge of the table, tipping from corner to corner.

'I think we should... *run!*' shouted McCools. He grabbed hold of Thumble Tumble's arm and started pulling her towards the door.

'*Ouch!*' screeched Thumble Tumble, scowling. 'Ouch, ouch, *ouch!*' she hollered again.

Dozens of cards were flying across the room like darts, with Thumble Tumble as the bullseye! Their sharp edges were slashing through her stripy tights into her shins.

She tried to swipe them away with her free hand, but

lost her balance and fell onto the floor. McCools grabbed hold of her other hand and pulled her back to her feet, dragging her towards the door.

She tried to pull her hand free to get her wand, but McCools' grip was too tight. The cards were now aiming at her arms and face as well as her legs. She was covered in gashes.

'Let go,' she shouted.

But McCools couldn't hear her from the noise of the cards zooming across the room.

'*Stop!*' she screamed at the top of her lungs.

McCools immediately let go of her arms and stood with his mouth wide open, staring behind her.

'How did you do that?' he eventually muttered.

'Do what?' she replied, picking herself back up off the ground.

'That!' he said, pointing behind her.

Thumble Tumble turned around to see a mass of playing cards suspended in mid-air.

'I don't know,' she said reluctantly. 'But I've got a feeling it's not permanent!'

The two of them turned and ran towards the door.

McCools jumped up and grabbed the door knob and the door swung open. They sprinted through into the hallway. As soon as Thumble Tumble crossed the threshold, the playing cards started searing towards them again.

She delved into her pocket and pulled out her wand. 'SEALISIUM!' she shouted, pointing the wand at the door. The door closed instantly, then began to rattle with the force of the playing cards thrashing into it from the other side.

'That was close,' gasped McCools.

'I'm not sure how long it will hold,' panted Thumble Tumble. 'Let's go!'

Buttercup was shivering. The room temperature was at freezing point. She couldn't feel her fingers or toes and the numbness had spread all over her body, completely immobilising her.

'*Why, why, why…* don't you want to come and play?' Silusa hummed as her translucent body wafted through the keyhole. 'I know you're in here. I just want to play,' she laughed.

Silusa went spinning around the room, tossing the furniture around as she went. With a nasty grin on her face, she flew over to the dolls' house, pulled it up off the ground and threw it across the room. As it came crashing down on the floor beside the bed, Buttercup's lame little body was tossed out.

'*Not fair*!' Silusa yelled like a petulant toddler at the sight of Buttercup lying unconscious on the floor.

'*I – wanted – to – play! wake up!*' she screamed into Buttercup's ear. But Buttercup didn't move. The tiny nymph barely had any life left in her.

Silusa was in such a rage, she did not feel the life forces of McCools and Thumble Tumble as they entered the room on their tiptoes. The dust and debris made it impossible for them to see Buttercup's tiny body.

Thumble Tumble held up her wand to conjure up a clearing spell, but McCools pushed the wand back down with his left hand, signalling to her to be quiet with his right.

The element of surprise was the only weapon they had, until they worked out how to use the cauldron!

They gradually made their way to the bottom of the bed and slipped under it. At last, they caught a glimpse of Buttercup. Thumble Tumble poked her head out for a better look.

'*You're it*!' Silusa's voice came pounding down from above her.

Thumble Tumble lay paralysed with fear. To her relief, Silusa drifted straight over her head and hovered above the rubble from the dolls' house.

'I can feel you,' Silusa grinned. 'I know you're close. And, you've got a puppy!'

Thumble Tumble and McCools realised simultaneously that the soot covering them must be acting like a coat of armour, making it impossible for Silusa to detect them.

Thumble Tumble immediately jumped up and ran towards Buttercup, scooping her little frame up into her arms. She sprinted towards the door as fast as her legs could carry her.

'Oh, poochy, poochy, poo!' Thumble Tumble could hear Silusa singing behind her. She glanced over her shoulder. Silusa was stroking McCools in her arms. The colour was all but gone from his fur and his eyes were grey.

Thumble Tumble placed Buttercup gently on the floor and yelled 'No!' at the top of her voice.

Silusa dropped McCools and raced over to her.

'*There* you are. I was wondering how long it would take you to rescue your mutt!'

'He's not a mutt,' Thumble Tumble retorted.

'Well, if a haggis isn't a mutt, I don't know what is!' Silusa cackled, suddenly diving forward and wrapping her arms around Thumble Tumble's waist.

Thumble Tumble tried to reach for her wand, but Silusa had her hands gripped tight.

'Shall we dance?' cackled Silusa, and without waiting for a reply she started cavorting around the room, with Thumble Tumble as her unwilling dancing partner.

The colour drained from Thumble Tumble's face and her teeth began to chatter as her body temperature plummeted in Silusa's chilly grasp. As she was twirled round and round, veins of blue frost began to stand out on Thumble Tumble's cheeks.

Silusa was determined to suck every drop of life force from her.

'One more squeeze,' murmured Silusa. 'That will do it!'

She clutched even more tightly around Thumble Tumble's body and pressed. There was a cracking sound. Silusa grinned at the thought of Thumble Tumble's ribs breaking!

Just then, a beam of light burned through Thumble Tumble's dress from the shattered cauldron. It rebounded off the opposite wall and continued in a criss-cross pattern across the room, weaving a spider's web of light.

The rays were shooting through Thumble Tumble, bringing warmth back to her body. The light beams were also penetrating McCools' and Buttercup's bodies, renewing their energy too.

McCools' fur turned brown, then auburn, before resuming its bright orange glow. By that time, Buttercup was fluttering a few inches off the ground.

Thumble Tumble looked around to see what was happening to Silusa. The beams of light were not penetrating her body. Instead, they were encapsulating her like a fly in a spider's web. The more Silusa tugged, the more the web bound her in.

The other Mantigh were now floating on either side of Silusa, trying to free her, but they too were entangled in the web. Within moments, all three of them were completely cocooned.

Thumble Tumble could just about make out the figure of a girl walking towards Silusa through the hazy mist. When the figure reached Silusa's cocoon, the two images merged into one with the most spectacular explosion. Particles of light erupted in a rainbow of colours.

When the sparks evaporated, the webs had disappeared, along with Silusa and the other Mantigh.

'Wh...what just happened?' stuttered Thumble Tumble.

'I don't really know,' said McCools, now back to his vibrant orange self. 'But whatever you did, it worked! I just hope the Buddhists aren't too miffed about their cauldron,' he added jokingly and winked over at Thumble Tumble.

## Chapter 19

## *Mogdred's Vow*

The fireworks display caused by the explosion set the sky ablaze outside the castle, blasting through the windows with bursts of pink, purple, blue and red cascading in every direction.

'Retreat! Retreat!' hollered Lumpsila as she fled with what was left of the sky patrol back into the clouds.

The ground troops were long gone. Bessie searched the castle gardens for Serena, but she too had bolted.

Bessie made her way back to the main entrance of the castle, where she was greeted by Isla and Jock.

'What happened?' she asked anxiously. 'Are they OK? Did they make it?'

'I'm not sure,' said Isla in a low voice. She pointed her wand towards the castle doors, ready to blast them open.

'Hold on!' cried Bessie. 'Look!'

A thin green strand of smoke was drifting under the massive doors. It made its way up and along the top, then suddenly the doors fell forward like a drawbridge. All that could be seen was a thick green cloud of smoke.

Then, through the smoke, the silhouettes of the escapees started to appear.

Thumble Tumble's A-line dress and pointy hat were the first things to materialise, closely followed by a much smaller, round ball shape with three pins sticking out the bottom.

Jock looked on nervously. 'Where's Buttercup?'

Thumble Tumble pointed up to her hat – and there, sitting on the rim, was Buttercup. She was still pretty weak from her ordeal, but alive! Bessie and Isla surged forward to hug Thumble Tumble, almost suffocating her in the process. She stumbled backwards from the weight of them bouncing off her, nearly tipping poor Buttercup off her hat.

'Let's get you lot home,' smiled Isla. 'We've got a party to go to.'

Two weeks later, and the birthday preparations were under way at last.

Lily had decided to postpone the party until Buttercup had fully recovered, which she had! Buttercup was back to her old self, organising everyone to within an inch of their lives. From her sick bed, she had even managed to arrange the table seating and order of songs for the dance.

The Flower Nymphs had gone to great lengths to make this party the best one ever. After all, they were no longer just celebrating Lily's birthday, they were now also celebrating Buttercup's escape and the defeat of Mogdred's army.

Hundreds of tiny fireflies, twinkling in the twilight, decorated the pond. In the gentle breeze, the surface of the water reflected the light from the fireflies, creating a rippling blanket of dancing stars.

The whole scene looked magical.

With the help of a colony of friendly worker bees, the nymphs had built a massive table made out of honeycombs. They then put so much food and drink on it, that you couldn't actually see the amazing structure they had created.

The centrepiece was a huge, seven-layer cake – one layer for each of the Flower Nymph clans. The bottom layer had white and yellow polka dots around the outside for the Daisy Clan. Then there was a layer hung with tiny azure bells for the Bluebell Clan, which was topped by a layer made from crushed ice for the Snowdrop Clan.

These were very carefully decorated. In contrast, the fourth layer was patchily covered in blobs of yellow and green icing. Blade had been in charge of this layer, which represented the Dandelion Clan. Normally this feisty little clan would have been up in arms at the insult, but they had decided to make an exception (just for today!).

The top three layers of the cake were made of yellow cupcakes entwined with thorny vines and finished with a single lily petal.

The magnificent centrepiece was surrounded by a host of other cakes, treats and sweets, from nectar tarts to dewdrop melts, all mouth-wateringly delicious.

On each of the corners of the table, the nymphs had placed a large jug. The jugs had spouts at the bottom instead of the top, but despite their unusual design, nothing was dripping out of them.

One jug, which contained honeydew, was being closely guarded by a grumpy bumblebee, who was not very eager to share it. He lunged forward with an angry buzz every time anyone even looked at it!

The tweezel berry juice and tulip sap jugs both had self-serve signs reading:

TOTALLY DELICIOUS,
SO PLEASE HELP YOURSELF.
BUT IF YOU ARE GREEDY,
YOU'LL BE THROWN OUT BY AN ELF!

The fourth jug was filled with bubbling waterfall mist. Beside it there was a little Water Fairy flying around frantically, calling out, 'Please drink responsibly.'

Four oversized toadstools had been placed at the top of the table for Thumble Tumble, McCools, Isla and Bessie, and a massive patch of grass had been cleared at the side for Jock.

The sounds from the band setting up on the left bank echoed across the pond. The frog baritones were croaking their scales as they marched up and down the side of the pond with their over-inflated chests sticking out below their neatly knotted black bow-ties. The grasshoppers were fine-tuning their back legs, using their highly sensitive antennae.

The air above the pond had been cordoned off with 'No Fly Zone' signs, as this is where the dancing would be taking place later.

Jock and Thumble Tumble were the first guests to arrive.

'Ooo, I'm thirsty,' said Thumble Tumble, and headed straight for the honeydew. She promptly turned around and took a glass of tulip sap instead. After coming face to face with Baxter the bumble bee, she had decided to give the honeydew a miss... for now!

'I can recommend everything except the honeydew.' She smiled over to Jock, who was already sampling treats from the table.

'Hi guys!' shouted a very excited Lily as she fluttered towards them with Blade in tow, his wings now fully functioning.

'Happy belated birthday,' said Thumble Tumble, handing Lily a parcel twice her size.

'Wow, what's this?' Lily asked. 'You really didn't have to,' she continued as she tore the wrapping paper off.

Inside was a tiny silver oven, complete with oven gloves.

'This is amazing!' she screamed excitedly, bobbing up and down in the air.

'To be honest, we were going to get you tweezel berry juice. But, we thought this might be better for keeping you lot out of trouble!' laughed Jock.

'What's all the hilarity?' asked Buttercup, zooming towards them from behind the band. She flew straight up to Thumble Tumble and gave her a big kiss on the cheek. She turned and did the same to Jock, who promptly glowed bright pink.

By eight o'clock the party was in full swing. Bessie and McCools were spinning in the air to the tune 'Pond by Moonlight', along with dozens of tiny fairies and nymphs. Although, they were so busy trying to avoid being bopped by the special guests, it was more of a 'duck and dive' than a 'swing and jive'!

Isla found herself deep in conversation with Baxter about why he was so angry all the time.

'Basically, it's because I really don't like sharing,' said Baxter.

'I see. Is this a new phenomenon, or have you always been selfish?' asked Isla.

'I'm *not* selfish,' snapped Baxter. 'I just don't like sharing,' he repeated, quite matter of fact.

Jock hadn't managed to drag himself away from the table as yet. So far, he had sampled every cake, sweet and drink (except the honeydew), and was now patiently waiting for the birthday cake to be cut.

The bouncer elves had been busy throwing out greedy fairies who had helped themselves to a bit too much of the buffet. They had considered approaching Jock a few times, but then thought better of it.

'He isn't *actually* being greedy,' said Tam, the biggest of the elves. 'He's just hungrier than everyone else!'

Buttercup had been waiting to get Thumble Tumble alone all evening. She spotted her chance as Bessie and McCools embarked on their next boogie. She fluttered over to Thumble Tumble and whispered in her ear. Thumble Tumble giggled, then got up and followed her into the bushes.

Mogdred was watching from the shadows. The air around her was cold and damp, and she hissed through her teeth at the happy scene in front of her.

Bessie, roaring with laughter as she twirled 'that' haggis around the fluttering bodies of Lily and Blade.

Isla, smiling at the boring conversation of a 'bumble bee'!

And Jock, looking sick-fully happy.

'His fat bottom hasn't left the table!' Mogdred growled.

Mogdred then turned her attention to Thumble Tumble.

'What are we up to, girls?' she mumbled as she surveyed her unsuspecting prey.

Buttercup and Thumble Tumble had gone to the back of the pond, where a little wooden bench stood on its own, surrounded by a bed of bright yellow flowers. Far away from the dancing lights and laughter, they could barely hear the band in the distance.

'This is my secret place,' whispered Buttercup, and she produced a tiny vial of bright yellow fluid and handed it to Thumble Tumble.

'The potion!' seethed Mogdred. 'How did that nymph get it out of the cauldron?

She clenched her fists so tight that her long black nails cut straight through her palms.

'It's about time you paid for what you've done to me, Thumble Tumble,' she said, as she unclenched her fist and pointed a long black finger towards Thumble Tumble's chest. 'You, and *everyone* you love,' she screamed.

The flash of light was blinding as the death bolt shot through the air and stabbed straight into Thumble Tumble's heart.

Everything went black...

The dungeon plunged into darkness as the huge oval mirror on which Mogdred had been watching her prey shattered, propelling shards of glass all over the dungeon floor.

Mogdred fell to her knees and threw her hands up to protect her eyes. They had started bleeding from the intensity of the light spawned by her own death bolt.

'Mark my words, Thumble Tumble,' she screamed as she writhed on the ground, 'I will have my revenge. Do you hear me? I-will-have-revenge!'

What's this?' asked Thumble Tumble as she twirled the little vial between her fingers.

'It's some of the potion from inside the cauldron!' said Buttercup, grinning.

'Take it... please.'

'But how did you get it?' Thumble Tumble asked.

'I'm afraid that will have to remain my little secret,' said Buttercup, tapping the side of her nose. 'Take it to the Buddhists. This will replace the potion you "borrowed" to save me. Besides, you don't want to make an enemy of the Buddhists, *or* their little friends, the Thistle Pixies! I have a feeling your paths will cross again... Protector!'

# Follow the adventure!

www.thumbletumble.co.uk
Find out more about this series, latest news, events and
when the next book will be available.

All books in the series can be ordered from the Thumble
Tumble website also available from your local bookshop
and online retailers.

Or by post from:
Thumble Tumble, PO Box 27132 Glasgow G3 9ER
Email:info@thumbletumble.co.uk

# About the Author

A.H. Proctor is a successful businesswoman, wife and mother who has unashamedly lived in a fantasy world for most of her life. Captivated from childhood by fairy stories and the world of the Brothers Grimm, her fertile imagination was held in check until she took her own young children to the beautiful and mystical Scottish Isle of Arran. When, one day, they asked her to tell them a story of witches and goblins, the floodgates opened.

*Thumble Tumble and the Cauldron of Undry* is the second book in a series of eight.

Don't miss the first book in the Thumble Tumble series, *Thumble Tumble and the Ollpheist*.